P. M. Hubbard and T.   ...der Room

›› This title is part of The Murder Room, our series dedicated to making available out-of-print or hard-to-find titles by classic crime writers.

Crime fiction has always held up a mirror to society. The Victorians were fascinated by sensational murder and the emerging science of detection; now we are obsessed with the forensic detail of violent death. And no other genre has so captivated and enthralled readers.

Vast troves of classic crime writing have for a long time been unavailable to all but the most dedicated frequenters of second-hand bookshops. The advent of digital publishing means that we are now able to bring you the backlists of a huge range of titles by classic and contemporary crime writers, some of which have been out of print for decades.

From the genteel amateur private eyes of the Golden Age and the femmes fatales of pulp fiction, to the morally ambiguous hard-boiled detectives of mid twentieth-century America and their descendants who walk our twenty-first century streets, The Murder Room has it all. ››

The Murder Room
Where Criminal Minds Meet

themurderroom.com

P. M. Hubbard (1910–1980)

Praised by critics for his clean prose style, characterization, and the strong sense of place in his novels, Philip Maitland Hubbard was born in Reading, in Berkshire and brought up in Guernsey, in the Channel Islands. He was educated at Oxford, where he won the Newdigate Prize for English verse in 1933. From 1934 until its disbandment in 1947 he served with the Indian Civil service. On his return to England he worked for the British Council, eventually retiring to work as a freelance writer. He contributed to a number of publications, including *Punch*, and wrote 16 novels for adults as well as two children's books. He lived in Dorset and Scotland, and many of his novels draw on his interest in and knowledge of rural pursuits and folk religion.

Flush as May
Picture of Millie
A Hive of Glass
The Holm Oaks
The Tower
The Custom of the Country
Cold Waters
High Tide
The Dancing Man
A Whisper in the Glen
A Rooted Sorrow
A Thirsty Evil
The Graveyard
The Causeway
The Quiet River
Kill Claudio

Picture of Millie
A London House Mystery

P. M. Hubbard

An Orion book

Copyright © Caroline Dumonteil, Owain Rhys Phillips and Maria
Marcela Appleby Gomez 1964, 2012

The right of P. M. Hubbard to be identified as the author of this work
has been asserted in accordance with the Copyright, Designs and
Patents Act 1988.

This edition published by
The Orion Publishing Group Ltd
Orion House
5 Upper St Martin's Lane
London WC2H 9EA

An Hachette UK company
A CIP catalogue record for this book is available from the British Library

ISBN 978 1 4719 0077 8

www.orionbooks.co.uk

CHAPTER ONE

'All right,' said Mrs Mycroft, 'you know the drill. If you see me wave my handkerchief, you must come out straight away, all of you, and come here. And if you want Daddy or me to come, wave your arms. Don't wave them unless you do, but if in doubt, wave. I'll be watching. And you keep your eye on me, in case I wave. Promise?'

'Promise,' said the biggest of the three children.

'All right. Go on then.' They were in fact already gone, running wildly towards the creamed edge of an almost level sea.

Paul Mycroft, flat on his back on the sand beside her, said, 'It's almost high tide, one of the smallest tides of the year. There is no wind at all. There is no sea. There is no under-tow or current. There are no sharks, as far as one can see or reasonably expect. I can reach the sea, if I have to, in about ten seconds from a lying start. It is a perfect day – the one day in the year when summer suddenly occurs. For heaven's sake relax and enjoy it. And let them enjoy it. And me.' He shifted the edge of his bathing trunks slightly where the sun had caught him the day before, scratched under it gingerly and sighed deeply. 'Peace, peace, peace,' he said. 'God knows I can do with a bit. Try some.'

'It's all very well, but we've got to have the drill. I can't be at peace unless I've closed all the gaps.'

'I know. Eternal vigilance. But it's done now. All the gaps are closed. Nothing can happen to any of us except sunburn and in due course, thank God, thirst. Lie down

1

and anticipate them with caution and hope respectively.' He rolled over on his towel and cocked an eye seaward. 'Look at those dinghies,' he said. 'You'd think they had motors. Not enough breeze to flap a handkerchief, and there they all are, lying over on their sides and running around like scalded cats. It's amazing.'

He completed his roll to his satisfaction and settled down comfortably on his face. 'But not for me. Too much like work on a day like this.'

'It's the young. They are energetic and competitive. And they love showing off.'

'Not only the young, you know. Look at old Leatherlegs – what's his name? – Dawson. Anybody's bronzed sea-daddy, all oilskins and far-seeing eyes. And I bet you he's out there, dashing about with the best of them.'

'He lacks a crew.'

'Millie Trent? She's probably back in time for the morning tide. Even Millie can't stay on the tiles indefinitely. I wonder what her story was this time?'

'How does she do it, Paul?'

'Get away with it?'

'Well, that too. But how does she manage it at all? I can give her – what? – eight years, to be charitable, and I'm sure I couldn't.'

He turned his head deliberately on his folded arms. 'Well,' he said, 'she's got a good figure and doesn't hesitate to make it apparent. But mainly she's keen, don't you see? Much too obviously for me. One has one's pride. And a sense of the ridiculous. I should have to be very drunk or very lonely to succumb to Millie. But for anyone who's not too choosey, or who isn't many people's cup of tea, or who's just plain in a hurry, she'd be all right.'

'I think it's horrible.'

'I think you're a bit jealous. Anyway, you asked. But

good Lord, you've seen plenty of Millies in your time. The world is full of them. It's only that in a respectable place like this she rather sticks out.'

'She certainly sticks out.'

'That's what I like about her. It warms my old bones. It's her mind that gets in my hair. Fancy being married to her.'

'I like the major.'

'Not really. You can't like a damned soul. You mean you feel sorry for him, or think he's harmless, or too good for her, or something. But you can't like a man in that case. And you can't think of him apart from it. I don't say he mayn't have been all right before she got at him, but you've got to take people as they are, not as they might have been.'

'No, but – if I met him casually, on a bus, say, I'd like him.'

'That would only be a first impression, and completely inaccurate as such. Unless you know he's the man who married Millie, you don't know him at all, only an abstraction. Anyhow, I don't think you'd be right. He's the hollow man, of course, poor sod, but there's things inside I shouldn't like. Good God, there's bound to be. Think what his life must have been these fifteen years past at least.'

'Why couldn't he divorce her?'

He rolled over on his back again. 'Why indeed? That's one of the things. Oh, to hell with Millie and the major.' He sighed and stretched deliberately and significantly. Mary turned and lay on her side, her face always to the sea.

The sun laid powerful motionless hands on her shoulders and back. The beach was silent and unbelievably empty. The three children made more noise than the Atlantic. Somewhere above them a pair of droning vapour trails headed westwards for America. They had come, with all their doubts and changes of mind, to the right place and at the right time. Peace, peace, peace. She shut her eyes and her head dropped on her arm.

Major Trent boarded the bus and said, 'I am the hollow man.' He raised his hat politely and looked at her with his little staring blue eyes. A gull said 'Kwee-ee' with a dying fall, and then came back again saying 'Kwee, kwee, kwee-ee' in a steady crescendo. Cathleen pulled at her sleeve and said, 'Mummy! Mummy!' in a unusually shrill voice, and the others joined in from a distance, 'Mummy! Mummy!'

She jerked upright and saw Paul already sitting up. They were on their feet together, and she counted, with sick relief, three distinct and identifiable figures racing towards them from the sea.

'Mummy,' said Cathleen, 'it's Mrs Trent.'

'Mrs Trent?'

'In the sea,' said Jennifer.

'She's floating,' said Cathleen. 'Her eyes are open, but she's quite white. Is she dead, do you think?'

Paul said, 'You stay here with Mummy.' He followed the children's tracks back to the edge of the sea, where the waves, hardly more than rounded ripples of clear water, followed each other gently on to the almost level sand. Ten yards out something lolloped disjointedly over the succeeding crests. It looked like seaweed with a white face.

Millie was in walking-out dress. She wore skin-tight sharkskin trousers, one white buckskin shoe and a sky-blue jersey which had shrunk into even more startling conformity with her figure. Her hair, despite her dinghy sailing, had not proved quite waterproof and her mouth gaped. Only her eyes, round, green and rather prominent, had the authentic Millie look. His first thought was for

4

the children, but there were no horrors. It was simply Millie in the water, unable to fend for herself. Paul, with some professional experience of bodies, had seldom seen one so inoffensive.

He took hold of the shoe and began to tow her ashore, but remembered that the children would be watching him. He left her to the waves again and walked up the beach. The children, clustered round Mary, stood wide-eyed but collected.

'Is she dead?' said Cathleen.

'She's dead,' said Paul. 'She must have fallen in the water and been drowned. Will you go up to the house,' he said to Mary, 'and phone for – the police, I suppose. Yes, the police – they'll do whatever's necessary. No need for a doctor.'

Mary said, 'You go straight up to the house, all of you. I'll catch you up before you get off the beach.' They went, hand-in-hand and rather reluctantly. She said, 'Was it all right? They don't seem upset.'

'Yes, all right. Nothing special to see, and they take the fact in their stride. You go and phone. I'd better stay and see she doesn't get up to any more mischief.'

'Oh Paul – you mustn't—'

'Nonsense. You know the way we were talking about her only a matter of minutes ago. Perfectly fair comment. It still is. I suppose she didn't like dying, but I can't see who else suffers. Go on up now, and I'll get her out.'

The buckskin shoe came off in his hand when he pulled at it. He wondered it hadn't followed its fellow. He put it on again, guiding the stockinged foot into the toe as he did with the smaller children. The action set Millie's head awash, but this did not seem to matter. Sea-water was clean, cleaner than Millie had been these many years. The moving waters at their priest-like task of rolling Millie up

the beach for decent burial. He got the shoe on to his satisfaction, almost asking 'Comfy?' automatically as he did
with the children. Then he took her by the ankle and towed
her gently on to the half-liquid sand, which the sea would
presently leave dry.

The body, which had had so much significance for every
man within sight of it, had been sterilised by death and
the sea. There was nothing, yet, for the gorge to rise at.
Everything looked exactly as it would have looked if she
had fallen into the water with her clothes on and climbed
out, laughing and making the most of their cling and
shrinkage. He could imagine it so clearly. Only this time
she had not climbed out. She had stayed in too long, and
the light had gone out, and now the body with its clinging
clothes meant nothing, nothing at all.

The face had changed. Millie's face had never been her
strong point, but then it had had other points of great
strength to contend with. It hadn't been a bad face in itself. Rather plump and highly coloured, with those green
cat's eyes and a mouth that was always smiling. He couldn't
remember, off-hand, ever seeing Millie not smiling. Now
he came to think of it, there was some virtue in this, however questionable the causes of her satisfaction. There
wasn't all that joy in the world, after all. He suddenly saw
that the face was pathetic. Poor Millie, quite chap-fallen,
with the laughter-lines drawn hard down the side of her
dropped mouth and her eyes seeing no further cause for
satisfaction in anything. He believed, as he had told Mary,
that no one was likely to suffer for her death, but he was
surprised to find himself suddenly very sorry for Millie.

The ambulance rolled discreetly on to the car-park behind the tamarisks and stopped by an ices-and-minerals
cabin not yet open for business. The driver got out a fold-
ing stretcher and came down the beach with a constable

in uniform. The constable's boots were beautifully polished, and he stepped delicately and unwillingly into the salt mushiness at the edge of the sea. He said, 'Mr Mycroft?'

'That's right. I asked my wife to phone you.'

'You found the body in the sea, sir?'

'The children found it, in fact, and called us. I brought it out of the water, as you see.'

'I understand you know the lady, sir – a Mrs Trent?'

'That's right. Staying with her husband at the Carrack Hotel. Major Trent.'

'Yes, sir. We've sent a car for him. Is there anything more you can tell me, sir?'

'I don't think there is really. She was floating about ten yards off-shore in the shallow water. She was obviously dead. I simply brought her in to make sure the tide didn't take her out again. It's on the turn.'

'Quite right, sir, so it is. All right, Joe. Better get her in the ambulance.'

' "Peace, peace, peace," says I,' said Paul later, ' "Nothing more can happen." And there was dead Millie creeping up on us out of the sea even while we were saying just what sort of a woman she was alive.' He raised his glass of bottled beer and stared through it at the midday sun. 'It hasn't put the children off the sea, I hope, has it?'

'I don't think so. They are determined to go down again this afternoon. I think they hope someone else will have come in by then.'

'Tell them the tide's out. Whatever their predilections in jetsam, they may as well get the facts of life right. Tide is more important than time hereabouts with the river running as it does.' He stretched himself in his cane verandah chair. 'I'm glad we took a house, aren't you? I know it means work, but fancy having the children at the Carrack, spitting out the hotel food and asking the wrong questions about Millie Trent.'

'I think so. A hotel would be nice for us for a bit, but not with the family. Where do you suppose Millie went in? She could swim, couldn't she?'

'I've never seen her at it. A bikini and sun-tan oil were more in her line. But yes, of course she must have been able to swim a bit. Even in these days of universal life-jackets no one would go dinghy sailing, surely, unless they could manage to paddle around till they were picked up. I suppose she could have gone in anywhere on either side of the river and been taken out by the night tide. It wouldn't have taken her very far as it is now. And then the morning flood brought her in and put her down on Lanting instead of taking her back up-river.'

'I wish it had put her down somewhere else, but I suppose the sooner the better, anyhow. Paul – there's nothing here to involve you professionally, is there? You are on holiday, aren't you?'

'Oh yes,' said Paul, 'I'm on holiday all right. With one small reservation, possibly, but that's nothing to do with Millie Trent. Don't worry. I remain a tripper, though the seas were choked with drowned Millies.'

'There are bound to be questions asked, though, aren't there? The major was looking for her yesterday evening. Someone must know where she was. At least, Millie being Millie, one tends to assume she wasn't alone.'

'One does indeed. Straight off the tiles into the river. I wonder if she was tight? Not that that was one of her vices. She could knock it back with the best, but I never saw her anything more than warmed up.'

The feet crunched hesitantly on the shingle path at the side of the house, and Paul shot to his feet. 'Trent, my dear chap, come in and sit down. I don't – there's nothing much one can say that it's any good saying. I'm going to give you a drink.'

Major Trent said, 'I came to thank you,' He blinked his small eyes quickly at them and sat awkwardly on the edge of a chair. He was immaculate as usual, immaculately casual in a blue blazer with a Paisley silk scarf tied stockwise in the open collar of a fine check shirt.

Mary said, 'We did nothing. We just happened to be there. I'm so sorry—'

Paul came back out of the house and handed him a glass. 'Drink that,' he said.

The major took it and lifted it vaguely in their direction. Paul thought he was going to say 'Happy days,' but he checked himself, failed to find a formula that suited the occasion and drank in silence. 'I've just come from the police station,' he said. 'They told me you found her. I – I thought I'd come here, not that damned hotel. And I wanted to thank you.'

'I'm glad you came,' said Mary. 'You must stay and have lunch with us.'

'That's very kind. I don't know. It's the shock, you see. Seems almost impossible to believe she's dead. She was always – full of life, Millie. And coming suddenly like this, it's very difficult to get hold of. You see that? I hope I'm not upsetting you. I'd better be on my way. Just wanted to thank you.' He drained his glass.

Paul said, 'You sit where you are and I'll get you another.' The major made no move. He sat there staring at Mary. His clipped ginger moustache trembled slightly, and she thought for a moment that he was going to cry. He said, 'I never thought it would be this way, do you see? I always assumed she'd outlive me. She was younger, you know – a good deal. I'm afraid I bored her at times. I can't think how she came to drown. She could swim – not much, you know, but enough to get ashore.'

9

He took the drink Paul gave him, repeated his silent gesture of incantation and drank deliberately. 'The trouble is, I don't know where she was yesterday. The police asked me, you see – well, they would, naturally. I had to say I didn't know. Sounds a bit off, though, doesn't it?'

He gazed into the amber heel of his glass, raised it and poured it down. 'I had asked one or two people, but I wasn't worried. She'd have told me when she came back, you see. And she hadn't been gone long. But now I don't know, and it sounds queer to say so. What do you think?' He looked sharply at Paul, but his eyes were not quite in focus. Paul wondered whether they'd given him something at the police station, or whether he had fortified himself before he left the hotel. They must, after all, have told him what had happened.

'I don't see it's anything to worry about,' he said. 'One can't always say where one's going or how long for. As you say, one explains it when one gets back.'

'That's it. That's it. I thought – well, I mean, it was nothing unusual, you see. And then to have this happen. I can't get over it. I couldn't believe it when they told me, and I still can't in a way. But I mean that's nonsense, you see. I've seen her. But it's the idea of it. I keep taking it for granted she'll be back.'

He stood up and moved into the sunlight, perfectly steady on his feet, but slightly breathless, as if he had been running. 'I mustn't stay,' he said. 'No, really, thank you, you're very kind, but I'd better be on my way. Thank you again.' He marched off, soldierly and immaculate, with six straight fingers of Paul's whisky inside him.

'He's shaken,' said Mary. 'Do you think we were wrong about nobody's being hurt but Millie?'

'Not really. He's odd, isn't he? I agree he's shaken. But—'

'People are when they win the pools.'

'Or when the X-ray is negative. Or when they're acquitted of murder. I know that. I don't for a moment think the major's heart is broken. The facts are all against it. But there was something a bit cagey about him, wasn't there?'

'The only thing I did wonder,' said Mary, 'was why he came here at all.'

CHAPTER TWO

'Well, sir,' said the sergeant, 'that seems to be about all you can tell us. And that's only to complete the record, really. Don't add much, do it?' He pushed the signed statement aside and sat back in his chair. 'You're not staying at the Carrack, are you, but I understand you know Major and Mrs Trent. Particular friends of yours?'

Paul looked at the massive face opposite and caught an answering gleam in the puckered eyes. 'No,' he said, 'oh no. Everyone knew Mrs Trent in a way, but we hadn't had much to do with them. We're rather – you know what it is with a family. We get someone to sit in with the children and go along to the Carrack for a drink or a dance occasionally, but we're not really in with the people staying there.'

'That's right. When you say everyone knew Mrs Trent—?' He put his head on one side and did not finish his sentence.

'Well – you couldn't miss her, you know. She was a pretty colourful character.'

'An attractive lady, they tell me. Always had plenty of attention.'

'Oh yes, she was attractive, all right.' He thought for a

11

moment. 'Look, sergeant, suppose you tell me what's worrying you. What I say isn't evidence, as you know, apart from what you've got on paper there, but I don't in the least mind telling you what I can for what it's worth. Only you must ask the questions.'

'Well, the truth is, we can't seem to find how she come to be in the water. She hadn't been in all that long – well, you know that, you saw her – and there doesn't seem to be any doubt she was drowned. But we can't trace her movements for – oh, nearly twenty-four hours or more before she come up on Lanting: and of course we've got to know, if only for the Coroner. Major Trent, now – he came down to see you, didn't he, after he'd been at the Station here? To tell the truth, that's why I asked if they were particular friends of yours.'

'Oh no. He did come to see us, as you say. He said he had come to thank us for what we did. He seemed shaken all right, but it was difficult to tell what he was really feeling. He didn't stay long. Drank a couple of stiff whiskies and took himself off.'

'Did he?' said the sergeant with a hint of wistful admiration. 'I give him a nice brandy straight here at the Station, because I thought he needed it. Nothing would have worried him much after that, would it now? But you know him that bit better than I do. How would you say he was taking it, apart from the shock, when you saw him?'

'Well – he wasn't broken-hearted, you know. At least, that was what we thought. Mrs Trent wasn't an easy woman to be married to, sergeant. But there it was, he'd been married to her all these years, and he couldn't get used to the idea that he wasn't any longer. His reaction wasn't the conventional one, but then it wasn't, at least to all appearance, a conventional marriage. He seemed worried that he couldn't tell you where she had been. But you see – well, one got the impression that he never did know where she was half the time. Of course, it's unusual, but you'd have thought he'd have got used to it by now.'

'Not much regard for appearances on either side, is that it?'

'Practically none. It was live-and-let-live carried to its ultimate conclusion. What everyone wondered, of course, was why they stayed married at all – if you like, why he didn't divorce her. But the front they preserved was admirable in its way. They behaved with perfect equanimity both to each other and about each other in public. It was an odd business.'

'He didn't try to – well, keep an eye on her at all?'

'Not at all, I don't think, no.'

'He said he had asked several people about her the day before. That's why I wondered.'

'Yes. Yes, now you come to mention it, I think he did. It hadn't struck me before, but when I come to think of it, it doesn't seem quite in character.'

'Would you say, now, that Mrs Trent had any particular fancy at the moment, sir? I mean, was she going round with anyone in particular during the last week or so?'

Paul considered the matter. 'Do you know,' he said, 'I think it would be misleading if I mentioned any names. What I mean is – I think it would simply be misleading to suggest anything in the way of the eternal triangle, with the motives and emotions usually attached to it. There couldn't be any eternal triangle with the Trents. It was more like a perpetual polygon.'

For a moment the sergeant's eyes opened wide and stared, sea-grey, into Paul's with a mixture of amazement and incredulity. Then he threw his head back and let out a bellow of laughter. A hatch in the side wall opened and a young constable looked through, gazed inscrutably at his superior for a moment and shut it silently. But the sergeant was not to be shaken.

'Mr Dawson, now,' he said, 'What about him, sir?'

'They'd been sailing together a lot, but everyone pairs off for that. And it takes a desperate man to make love, even to a Mrs Trent, in a twelve-foot dinghy, sergeant.'

'But he'd been seeing a lot of her?'

'My dear chap, he'd probably seen all there was to see, but so had a lot of other people. I must try to make you understand that. I know it's not usual. Millie Trent really was a little friend of all the world. If you're thinking of foul play – and obviously it's your job in a case like this, whatever the evidence – I just don't think it's any good your thinking along the usual lines of jealousy, resentment and so forth.'

'Not so far as the husband is concerned, perhaps, sir. I grant you it's unusual, but it may be so in this case. I don't know yet. But there's always the others. There may be one less disposed to take things lightly, if you see what I mean.'

'A Bywaters who vents his jealousy on Mrs Thompson instead of her husband?'

'Ah,' said the sergeant, 'you're interested, I can see. That sort of thing, perhaps. A younger man, let's say, who gets caught up with this easy-going lady and can't bear to find, as he's sure to do sooner or later, that so far as she's concerned he's just a – a routine job, so to speak. What about that, now?'

'Yes,' said Paul, 'I grant you that. That's an interesting speculation. And I suppose it could happen. But I can't give you the least shred of evidence that it did. At least, I never saw any follower of hers that looked the least likely to harbour any illusions of that sort. That's not to say, of course, that one didn't exist. But I can't help you with him.'

14

'Not, of course,' said the sergeant, 'that we're looking for evidence of foul play. I'm relying on your discretion a lot as it is, sir—' Paul bowed his acknowledgements and assurances – 'but I particularly wouldn't want it getting around that we're on that tack. The fact is, we're not. But it's all so wide open that we've got to consider all the possibilities.'

'Yes, of course. But in fact – I mean, she could swim a bit, but not much, and she was fully dressed – by her standards, anyway. If she'd fallen in somehow at half-tide, with the river running in or out the way it does, it's not impossible, surely, for her to have been carried away and lost her head? You know as well as I do, it's keeping or losing your head that does it. If you're content to swim steadily across the tide and not worry about how much you're being carried up or down, as the case may be, it's not difficult to get ashore somewhere. But if you panic and waste a lot of energy trying to get back to the point you went in at, anything can happen. There's not much of a tide now, as you know – we're getting near full neap – but there's still plenty of flow up and down river for all that, and there are always the bad places where it tends to sweep out a bit.'

The sergeant looked at him. He said, 'What makes you think she went in up the river, sir?'

'What? Well I'm hanged. I think I just assumed it. I assumed she went in at Pelant or somewhere near it. Do you mean you don't think she did?'

'We can't say for certain, of course. But it doesn't look like it. It's the way the currents set, as you know, sir. If she'd gone down river with the tide, she'd more likely have come in on Bree Sands or even at Skittle Cove. But coming in on Lanting as she did, the chances are she come from up the coast a bit. Not far, of course. Bartenny way, that sort of thing. And there's no one to say she went there, let alone what she was after if she did. That's our difficulty, sir.'

'Lor,' said Paul, 'that is odd, isn't it?' He thought for a moment. 'There is one thing,' he said. 'It'd be much easier for her to fall in a bit along the coast than up river. If she'd been scrambling on the cliffs this side of Bartenny, looking for a quiet spot, perhaps, or a gull's nest or something, she could have gone down into deep water easily enough, and it wouldn't be easy to climb out. There wouldn't be the tide-run to contend with that she'd have in the river, but it would be much lonelier and more frightening, and the result could have been the same.'

'Quite right, sir, so it could. And that may be what happened. But I must confess I'd like to know which particular gull's nest she was looking for. We haven't had any fellow bird-watcher come forward so far, and I don't expect we will. But you'd think somebody would have seen her go, if she walked along the cliff path, that is. Of course, she may have covered her tracks deliberate. Or she may have gone up the road to the shops and then cut across towards the head, around the back of Lanting. Or of course she could have gone by boat, but in that case somebody must know more than they're saying, and the chances are much stronger that she'd have been seen. No, my bet is that she went overland by herself, though I don't doubt she was expecting to meet someone when she got wherever it was she was making for. That someone must know she was going, one would think, but that's not to say he knows any more. They may not have met, you see. She may have run into trouble on the way and never kept the appointment, if there was one. Then, whoever it was she was meeting found she didn't turn up and simply came away. He'd have heard later what happened to her, but if he hadn't even seen her and wasn't keen that their appointment should be known, as very likely he wasn't, there isn't really much call on him to come forward. Of course, if she'd had her head bashed in and we were looking for a murderer, this chap would probably come forward to protect himself, in case their arrangement to meet came out later. But there's nothing like that. In fact, there's really no call for anyone to say anything, and in all the circumstances I reckon nobody will. We'd like to know a bit more, naturally, but even we've no cause to worry ourselves overmuch about it.'

'No, I know. Still, it doesn't stop one wondering, does it? There'll be an inquest, I suppose?'

'Friday, that is. It'll be an open verdict, unless something unexpected turns up before then. But of course we'll go on keeping our ears open. There's one thing, sir. You say you're not one of the hotel regulars, but you probably know most of them and see them occasionally. If anything comes your way, you might let me have it, unofficial like. There's bound to be talk, any amount of it, and if anything significant is said, I'd like to know of it. And you will keep this conversation to yourself, sir, won't you? We don't want to make a mystery where there mayn't be one, do we? That's why I don't want me or my chaps asking too many questions among the Pelant lot. But you'll hear as much in a day, I reckon, without asking as we should if we stood the place on end for a week.'

'I'll listen,' said Paul, 'but I don't guarantee any results. In any case, you have my absolute assurance that I won't repeat anything you've said, or suggest that you have said anything at all beyond the formalities.'

'That's right, sir, and we'll be very grateful to you. I hope this won't be spoiling your holiday.'

'Oh no – gives one something to think about.'

'And the children are not too upset? Must have been a bit of a shock for them, finding her like that.'

'To tell you the honest truth, I don't think they'd have missed it for the world. There wasn't anything nasty to see, and children are very matter-of-fact about things like that. Haven't you found that?'

'Ah, to tell you the truth, sir, so I have. It's the parents won't have it. You'd be surprised what we see sometimes – children as calm as battery-birds and the parents having hysterics on their behalf. It makes you wonder who ought to be in charge. Well, good-day to you, sir, and thank you.'

Paul looked at his watch as he came out into the road. Not too much of the morning gone, and the weather still, miraculously, as good as ever. He should be able to find the family in time for a swim before lunch. He set off quickly through the straggle of shops and bungalows that formed the upper, newer and more regrettable part of Pelant. He passed Pike's General Stores, Pike's Café and Tea-Rooms and the Pelant Motor Egineering Company (J. R. Pike, Proprietor). He was never quite sure which was the original foundation or who among their executives was the head of the family, but J. R. Pike was evidently doing good business in all his capacities.

By the garage he turned right into a roughly metalled lane that picked its way through the holiday accommodation until it turned into a sandy track bordered with tamarisks, and ran out round its last bend into the designated car-park wedged between the grass-covered dunes and the silver shelving sweep of Lanting Bay.

There were more people down today. The car-park had a dozen cars in it, but their passengers, scattered over the great stretch of sand, did little to mar the effect of space and sunlight. Across the wide river-mouth Skittle Hill stood up blunt and green above the silver streak of the

Cove. On his right the jumbled dunes rose higher and higher till they merged in the broad swell of grass and heather that climbed steadily to the weathered crags that topped Bartenny Head. That was the way Millie might have gone – what? – three days ago now. He imagined that small, vital figure, dark blue legs and pale blue top, padding quickly up the long green slope, busy in its perpetual quest for joy and wholly unconscious of a menace that must have lurked somewhere among the rocks ahead.

What the hell? he thought. Millie dead was better than Millie sick or Millie old. He had seen too many ageing Millies, hard faced, with all the joy dried out of them, to regret the sudden dousing of this small flame.

'You've been a long time,' said Mary. 'You're sure you're not getting involved?'

Paul said, 'If it's any comfort to you, I told the sergeant I was an Inspector of Taxes. That's a criminal offence, though I reckon a venial one. But he's an interesting chap, and we had quite a talk.'

'Thank goodness for that. The children were getting impatient, so I let them go in. There they are, next to the immense leathery man in a sort of male bikini.'

Paul picked out the three fast moving figures at the edge of the placid sea. 'I'll join them,' he said. 'What about you?'

'I'll come presently. Let me relax for a bit now you've relieved me. Do they know yet how Millie got in the water or where she was?'

'I gather not. No one knows anything. There's an inquest on Friday, and I suppose something may come out then. But I get the impression that they don't know any more than they did.'

Mary frowned. 'Someone must know. They may not know how she got in the water, but someone must know

19

where she was. I suppose they don't want it known she was with them. That's natural enough.'

'Yes. I bet there's some hard explaining going on in the married quarters. "But I told you, dear, don't you remember, I just took the car into Clanbridge to get some tobacco and a haircut." Now don't look at me like that. You know where I was all that day, and I can call three highly dependent witnesses to prove it.'

'Oh go and get in to the sea and leave me in peace.'

He stepped into his bathing trunks and walked down towards the children. The air was cool and soft on his skin, and he felt the conscious glow of virtue that comes for no known reason from the successful beginnings of a sun-tan. The children screamed to him, and he waved absently, his eyes on the green curve of cliff to his right. Half-way up the slope a small soldierly figure, dark blue above and pale grey below, marched steadily up the coast-guard's path towards the jagged outline of Bartenny Head.

CHAPTER THREE

A man Paul had never seen before came out of the hotel and crossed the narrow road to the yacht-club hard. He wore canvas shoes and scarlet shorts, turned up to make them even shorter. His legs, hirsute and stringy, were innocent of sunburn and still showed, like the fetter-gall on a convict's ankles, the marks of habitual sock-suspenders. His roll-necked sweater had reindeer knitted into it and a yellow plastic life-jacket laced over it. He was topped out with a stocking cap in green and white rings. He had a knowing smile on his face and the sea in his blood.

At home, thought Paul, he was probably a respectable

professional chap who wore a dark suit to the office. A perfectly pleasant, harmless chap, no funnier than the winter-sports enthusiast, and much less sinister than the week-end horseman, because his snobbery had no social overtones. He was even, like all enthusiasts, a little endearing, though slightly daunting. He disappeared down the hard, hailing someone unseen and waving a furled sail.

Given the right tide at the right time of day, the yacht-club hard was always worth watching. There must have been fishermen here once, tending their gear because their lives depended on it. They still in fact existed, but at this time of the year they had other fish to fry. The sailing folk were earnest all right, but with a different quality of earnestness.

He put his tankard on the weathered stone and leant over the wall, idly amused in the soft sunlight. The majestic blue curve beside him dawned slowly on his consciousness. 'Hullo, Susan,' he said. 'I didn't see you.'

She was watching the nautical ants' nest below inscrutably. Her mouth at the best of times was a little sulky. He supposed she was seventeen, but young for her age. 'Oh, hullo,' she said.

She did not turn her head and he saw that she was watching her father. He was bronzed and boyish, his hair cut so short that you could not see whether it was sun-bleached or grizzled. He was rallying in a clipped, military voice the extremely pretty girl who bent with him over the varnished sides of a racing dinghy.

'Not sailing today?' said Paul.

She shook her lank hair. She said, 'No,' in a completely colourless voice. Then she roused herself and said elaborately, 'Pam's crewing for Daddy. She's done a lot. They're racing this morning.'

Paul, who rent his heart daily for the short-lived griefs

of his own daughters, wondered how he would be able to bear it when they were seventeen, conspicuous in sky-blue and defenceless as young whales. He said, 'To my mind you're well out of it, but I don't expect you think so.'

She turned and fixed him with a pair of pale green eyes that startled him with their sudden maturity. 'As a matter of fact,' she said, 'I think so, too, but I feel I oughtn't to. I ought to be resentful, and in a way I am, but I'm so relieved inwardly it isn't true. And then I feel ashamed of feeling like that. It's a bit complicated, actually.'

'Oh Lord, yes,' said Paul. 'I know. My father was a fisherman. I don't mean this sort of stuff.' He waved a hand vaguely down river. 'I mean flies and waders. I got cold and bored – God, how bored I got – and the more bored I got, the guiltier I felt. It isn't fair.'

Susan said, 'I'm not bored, I'm scared. I feel sick every time the boat heels.'

'Does your father know, do you think?'

Her eyes were down on the hard again. She said, 'I expect so, but it wouldn't do to say so.' She straightened up, turned her back firmly on the hard and heaved herself up on to the wall, facing the hotel. 'I expect I'm not the only one. In fact, I know I'm not – wasn't. Mrs Trent was scared stiff. I bet you wouldn't have guessed, though.'

'Mrs Trent? Was she? I'd never have guessed, no. How do you know, Susan?'

'She said so.' Susan twisted a minute pink handkerchief round her fingers. 'One didn't have to pretend anything with her. I liked her. I can't bear her being dead and everyone being lousy about her. She was worth a dozen of most of them – to me, anyhow. But of course it wouldn't do to say that either.'

'I'm sorry,' said Paul. 'I've been lousy about her myself. She did rather ask for it, you know. But of course I didn't really know her. Or only what everyone else knows.'

'I know. She ran around with all the men. But whose fault was that, anyway? Daddy makes horrible jokes about her, but you should have seen him looking at her when she came down to breakfast in the morning. Eyes on stalks. That's if Mummy wasn't down yet.'

'Golly,' said Paul, 'save me from my daughters. Mine are young yet.'

Susan smiled at him suddenly, and he saw with surprise that one of these days she was going to have tremendous charm. 'You wait,' she said. She turned towards the river again as the dinghy tacked smartly out between the moored boats, her father and the exquisite Pam flinging themselves neatly and economically from side to side in skilled harmony. 'I'm very fond of Daddy,' she said, watching him go. 'You understand that, don't you? But so far as Mrs Trent's concerned, they're all alike. She just happened, in fact, to be rather nice.'

'Yes. Yes, how little one knows. Do you mind telling me what people are saying? But don't worry if it upsets you.'

'I don't mind. Oh, the usual thing. That she went off to meet some man, and was probably tight, and not much of a swimmer anyway, and just slipped in and panicked, and serve her right. More or less that, anyway.'

'But where, do they think?'

'I don't know. Somewhere up-river.' She looked at him again, very directly. 'Do you mind telling me something?'

'I'll try. What is it?'

'You found her, didn't you?'

'Yes.'

'What was she wearing?'

'Slacks and a jersey.'

'No life-jacket?'

23

'Oh no. Why?'

'I just wondered.'

'Please tell me, Susan. It might be important.'

'Only – well, what I said. She was terrified of the water. She'd never have gone anywhere near it, where there was the slightest risk of falling in, without wearing her jacket. She told me she never did. Of course, she bathed, but she never did much more than get her feet wet. And that was on sand.'

Susan spoke without hesitation or contempt. She seemed to have no illusions about Millie. Paul said, 'But you liked her?'

'Oh yes. I told you, she was nice to me.'

'He was my friend,' Paul quoted, 'faithful and just to me.'

'Yes, but not only that.' Virginal, massive in sky blue, Susan turned to him. 'Don't you see? We had so much in common.'

'I see,' said Paul; and then, looking into the pale un-deviating eyes, 'At any rate, I'm trying to see. But what you mean is that when she went off on Wednesday – it was Wednesday, I suppose? Yes, it must have been – wherever she was bound for, it wasn't the sea. If it had been, she'd have had her life-jacket with her. Is that right?'

'Yes, that's right. Only as a matter of fact, I thought she had.'

'Do you mean you saw her go off to wherever it was?'

'I don't know that. I saw her go out towards the golf-course on Wednesday. She may have come back.'

'When was this?'

'Very early in the afternoon. Most of them hadn't finished lunch. I've been missing lunch, and I was up at the top of the path, where it opens out through the gorse bushes. I was reading. She came up the path wearing what you said and carrying her jacket.'

'Did she see you?'

'Oh yes. She called out to me. She said what a heavenly day it was. She seemed thrilled with everything. She always did.'

'Did you tell anybody you'd seen her?'

'Me? No, why on earth should I?'

'I heard that Major Trent was asking about her that evening.'

'Doesn't sound likely. Anyway, he didn't ask me. And even if he had, what could I say? I'd only seen her leaving. I didn't know where she'd gone or who she'd been with. I suppose she was with somebody, or going to be, anyway. But I don't know who.'

She looked over her shoulder. The dinghy, distinguishable now only by its sail number, was running goose-winged up-river before the mild westerly breeze, making for the start. She turned and sat with her hands between her tight blue knees, twisting the pink handkerchief over and over in her fingers. 'I wish we could go home,' she said.

'Why not ask?'

'With the weather just right for sailing and Pam here? That would be popular, wouldn't it?'

'Couldn't you go alone?'

'Of course I could, but I can't ask.'

'No. Look, if the hotel gets a bit much for you, come out and see us. Mary would love to have you, and Cathleen would be thrilled.'

'Couldn't I look after them for you for a bit? Give you and Mary a chance to get out and get me away from the hotel? Mummy couldn't be sombre about it if I was doing my good deed.'

'I think that sounds excellent. I must ask Mary officially, of course, but she'll jump at it. The family can be a nightmare, but I expect they'll be good with you at first. They are with anyone.' He finished his beer and turned towards the hotel. He said, 'Keep going, Susan. Nothing lasts.' She nodded, green-eyed, through her curtain of hanging hair. He crossed the road and went to the reception desk.

'Is Major Trent in the hotel?'

The girl's clothes, hair and make-up were pure Mayfair, but her voice was barely modified local. The effect was disconcerting and altogether charming. She said, 'I can't say for sure. I'll just find out for you.' She went off down the hall, lily-slender on her fantastic heels. When she came back, she said, 'He's in his room. Number 23. Shall I tell him then?'

'No,' said Paul, 'don't worry. I'll go up and knock. He needn't see me if he doesn't want to.'

The Carrack had never been anything but a mainly holiday hotel. There was no waterside pub hidden somewhere in the ground-floor back. It looked, and was, Edwardian with recent additions. It was the sailing that had put candles on the dining-room tables and the staff into starched white coats. It was still mainly seasonal, but in its peculiar middle-class way it was now fashionable. The corridors were painted white and the room numbers lacquered brass.

Paul knocked on the door of Number 23 and a voice inside said, 'Hullo?' He put his head round the door.

Major Trent had been standing with his hands in his pockets looking out of the window. He had turned his head but otherwise had not moved. Even when he saw Paul he remained for a moment frozen there, shoulders a little hunched, his eyes staring slightly above the craned neck.

Then he said, 'Hullo, Mycroft. Come in.' He turned his head to the window again. Paul shut the door behind him. It was the old-fashioned hotel's idea of a double bed-room, with two windows in a generous frontage and twin beds backed against the opposite wall. The dressing-table between the windows was still stacked with dead Millie's hunting-gear, but the bottles were sealed and the scent already faded. The major's things were ranged, very limited and orderly, on the top of a chest-of-drawers. They smelt of nothing. One bed was sealed down under a candle-wick bedspread. The other was neatly stripped but un-made. A used breakfast tray stood on the table between them.

'My fault,' said Major Trent. 'I haven't been downstairs yet, and they probably don't want to disturb me. Nice of you to come up.'

'Look,' said Paul, 'this wasn't what I came to ask, but would you like Mary to give you a hand?' He looked round the room, divided so neatly and decisively into two autonomous territories, the one still sovereign, the other evacuated and not yet reoccupied. 'If you'd like her to help pack your wife's things—'

'No. No, it's very nice of you, but don't worry. I'll get it all away presently. I can't go until Friday anyway, you see. There's the inquest.'

'I see. Yes, I'm sorry.' He joined the major at the window. The river was alive with dinghies now, and the babel on the hard had subsided. As he looked, Susan heaved herself off the wall and walked slowly across the road to the hotel.

'Frayne's girl,' said Major Trent. 'Comes here every year. I don't think if I were Frayne I'd leave her ashore and take another girl racing. But she may not mind.'

Paul said, 'She was a friend of your wife's, Susan. I think she's a bit upset by everything.'

Major Trent flicked his blue eyes at him sideways. 'Was

27

she? Yes, I think I did see them talking once or twice. The mother's not much use to a girl, I don't fancy. Too full of her own troubles. I'm glad Millie made friends with her. She was always kind, you know, Millie.'

'Yes,' said Paul. He hesitated, but found nothing to add. He had told the sergeant that Millie had been a little friend of all the world, but he had not meant it kindly. Now for the second time that day he felt himself rebuked. He said, 'There's one thing. I hope you won't mind my asking.'

'Go ahead,' said Major Trent. He did not turn round.

'Mary lent your wife a scarf. She wouldn't want to mention it herself, but I gave it to her, and it's a bit special. Do you think I could possibly have it?'

'Of course. What's it like? You know it, do you?'

'Oh yes. Black. It may not be here, and if so, please don't worry, but—'

'Have a look.' He jerked his head backwards. 'That cupboard there and the drawers under the dressing-table.'

The unoccupied territory, that went with the covered bed and the sealed bottles. The major did not move from the window.

Paul said, 'If you really don't mind—'

He ran the drawers out perfunctorily. The smell of Millie was stronger here, but everything was very orderly. Only the top drawer had some scarves, none of them black. He hesitated over them, hardly conscious of the fact that the scarf he was looking for did not exist. He shut the drawers and walked over to the cupboard. Here were clothes hanging he actually remembered, and Millie stepped out to meet him more vividly. The shoes were neatly ranged in pairs on the floor of the cupboard. On top of them, folded down unevenly in a corner, was a yellow plastic life-jacket. One edge lay across the toe of a black

28

satin shoe, and he saw the spread stain where moisture had run off the jacket.

He shifted a few things and looked vaguely round inside the cupboard. He knew Major Trent had not moved. He stooped and dragged a forefinger over the shiny surface of the jacket. Then he shut the cupboard and turned round. 'No,' he said, 'I don't see it, but for goodness' sake don't worry. Mary hasn't thought of it, I don't think. It was only my idea and it's of no real importance.'

The major stirred himself and turned away from the window. 'Sorry,' he said. 'If I find anything of the sort, I'll let you know.'

'Please forget about it. It really doesn't matter.'

'I'm going down. Want to get out for a walk, now the place is quieter. Wait a moment, and I'll come down with you. That's if you don't mind.'

'Of course.'

The major surveyed himself seriously in a small glass on the chest-of-drawers. He ignored the dressing-table mirror altogether. He picked up one hair-brush and smoothed down one side of his head. Then he passed himself fit for parade and joined Paul at the door. 'After you,' he said.

They went downstairs in silence, through the hotel lounge and out into the road. The heat was steady now, and the breeze had fallen away to almost nothing. Perfect weather, but not exciting sailing.

'You going up the village?' Major Trent asked. 'I won't keep you. I'm going out over the golf-course, I think. Thank you for coming. I don't like coming downstairs, that's the truth.' He smiled tightly, but his eyes blinked fiercely at Paul as if challenging him to see anything funny in it.

'Yes, I can understand that. Let me know if there's anything we can do.'

'I will. Thank you.' The major turned and walked steadily up the curving path towards the gorse bushes. Paul saw him out of sight and then turned up the road towards the shops. He put his forefinger in his mouth and licked it. It was scurfed with salt.

CHAPTER FOUR

As Paul opened the door, Mrs Dawson said, 'You know perfectly well we can't go home now. That would look worse than anything. And I've had enough to put up with this last week as it is.'

He checked at the harshness of her voice and then, seeing there was nothing else he could do, pushed the door wide open and walked into the room. Jack Dawson sat facing him, hunched in a low chair. His feet were straddled and his knees pressed together with his hands clasped between them. He had been staring at the floor and now looked up at Paul under drawn brows, without moving his head. He looked abject.

Paul said, 'Oh, I'm sorry—' and Dawson said, 'Oh, hullo, Mycroft' simultaneously. Mrs Dawson sat straight up, her hands clutching the arms of a wheel-backed chair. She looked from one to the other and said nothing. She had none of her husband's pretensions to youthfulness.

'Not a bit, come on in,' said Dawson. 'We were discussing plans, but it's time we had a drink. I'll see if Charles has opened up next door.' He got up as if the air above his shoulders was of an intolerable weight. His wife said, 'You have a drink if you want to. I'm going upstairs.'

Paul held the door for her and she went out ungracefully

without acknowledgement. When he turned, Jack Dawson had found his sea-legs again. He gave Paul a quick gleam of puckered eyes and almost shrugged. He said, 'I don't know about you. I need a drink.'

'I've come to fetch Susan Frayne. She's baby-sitting for us, bless her. But I'm much too early. Yes, I'll join you certainly.'

Charles was behind the bar reading the *Nicomachean Ethics* in Greek. He lifted his noble brow and said, 'Good evening, Mr Dawson. Good evening, Mr Mycroft.' He wore a starched white jacket and in the intervals of his struggle with Greats gave an immaculate professional service.

Jack Dawson chose rum and shepherded Paul back into the next room. He settled himself in the chair his wife had just left and delivered himself of the inevitable opening line. 'Women are the devil,' he said.

Paul, who habitually allowed his curiosity to outrun his good taste, looked knowing and sympathetic and waited. Dawson gulped his rum and said, 'Been having a flaming row, as a matter of fact, just before you came in. About Millie Trent, God rest her soul. Funny having a row with one's wife about a woman who's dead. I suppose it's been boiling up.'

'That's right,' said Paul. 'That's the way it happens.' His own rows with his wife were invariably the result of momentary mutual exasperation, but he had no wish either to disclaim relevant experience or to start a general discussion of matrimonial relations.

'I have been seeing a lot of Millie, of course. She was wonderful in a boat, you know. And Agnes doesn't care for it.'

Paul thought, 'Agnes, my goodness.' He said, 'She's probably a bit nervous and doesn't like to say so. I think

31

a lot of women are.'

'Could be. She's never said so. But Millie was wonderful. Very quick and as cool as a cucumber. And always
seemed to enjoy it in all conditions. Like having a man in
the boat.'

Paul, off-hand, could think of nothing less like a man
than Millie, in or out of a boat, but said nothing. Dawson
finished his rum and stared in vague frustration into the
empty glass. 'As a matter of fact,' he said, 'it's not quite
true that it's been simmering until now. We had one row a
few days ago. Agnes went pretty well off the deep end
about her then. I had to say I wouldn't sail with her any
more. Could you do with another? I'm having one.'

'A small one. I don't want to take Susan home in a cloud
of alcohol.'

Dawson disappeared into the bar and brought back a
small gin and a second monumental rum. 'Thanks,' said
Paul. 'That seems a pity when she was so good in a boat.'

Dawson gulped half his rum and said, 'It was a bloody
shame.' His voice had thickened suddenly, and Paul wondered whether he had started the evening earlier from a
private supply. 'I don't know,' said Dawson. 'I don't see
– Millie was marvellous company, do you see? I felt on
top of the world all the time I was with her. That was
what upset Agnes. She knew that. But I don't see she had
a right to object. Do you?'

He opened his eyes wide and stared at Paul, bronzed
and grizzled, with the face of a deprived child. Paul said,
'Not really. But I suppose it's natural. It depends, I
suppose—'

'There was nothing else, actually.' He groped for words
and lapsed suddenly into racing terms. 'There was no
infringement, do you see? The objection couldn't be
sustained. I'd have – I wanted to, of course. Millie was

32

damned attractive, out of the boat. But she wouldn't play. I don't know why. And now she's dead. I feel bloody low, I can tell you.'

Paul said, 'I think a lot of people miss her.' He was conscious of a sudden uncomfortable sincerity.

'I can't think how it happened. If she'd been out with me on Wednesday she'd have been all right. As it was, I sailed single-handed. There was no racing, of course. Agnes said she'd help me get the boat in. She can do that. But I can't think how Millie came to get in the water. There was nothing outside bar a fishing-boat or two. I tell you, I feel bloody awful about it. Sorry I'm burdening you like this. Do you think we might have one more?'

'Not for me,' said Paul. 'It's up to you. If I were you I shouldn't. It's not going to make you feel any better.'

'All right. I suppose not. Only I was feeling low and felt I needed a stiffener. In actual fact, it was that that started the row with Agnes. She resented my feeling like this. I didn't wave it at her, of course, but she spotted it. They always do. Then like a fool I suggested our cutting our stay short and going home. That tore it. Couldn't I enjoy Pelant without Millie around? And what about her? I was supposed to be on holiday with her, not Millie. They always say the same thing. They know they've got you cold, because you can't give them the true answer, and anything else they can tear to pieces. And I keep thinking that if it hadn't been for that first bloody row, or if I'd had the guts – Oh well, what the hell?'

He got up and looked at Paul with sudden wariness. He showed none of the physical symptoms of alcohol. 'I'm sorry,' he said. 'Shouldn't be saying all this. You'll keep it to yourself, will you?'

'Of course. I'm sorry there's nothing I can do.'

'That's right. There's nothing anyone can do. Only forget all about it. Including this outburst. You'll do that, won't you, there's a good chap?'

'I will of course.'

Dawson nodded. He said, 'I'd better go upstairs.' His voice was completely toneless. He made for the door, forcing his way almost visibly against impalpable pressures. Paul opened the other door and went into the bar.

There were still no other customers. Charles was busy with Aristotle, but he was on his feet before Paul was well through the door. He said, 'Something else, Mr Mycroft?'

'No thank you, Charles. I'm picking up Miss Frayne, but I'm still early. I'll wait if I may. Mr Dawson has gone upstairs.'

Charles said, 'That's right.' He balanced the tone so delicately that Paul could not decide whether he was agreeing with the statement or approving the action.

'I'm afraid he's upset.'

'We all are,' said Charles. He was perfectly in earnest, stating an observed fact without sentimentality or ridicule.

'I should not have said all.'

'I think so. You said upset, Mr Mycroft. You didn't say grieved or regretful. Not everyone regrets Mrs Trent's death, certainly, but we are all disturbed by it. Most of us, of course, do regret it very much.'

'Yes. I'm sorry. I should have been more exact in my terms. If you don't mind my saying so, I should not have expected to find you among her admirers.'

'Ah, but—' His tone was almost angry, but he checked himself and made a fresh start. 'I'm sorry,' he said. 'I didn't in fact find her particularly desirable – not to me personally. I think that's what you meant, isn't it? I don't think I could have got over the barrier of doubtful taste. But she was full of delight, you know. Something much more nearly universal than mere sex. φιλομμειδὴς Ἀφροδίτη.

He gave the words an unfamiliar pronunciation, which Paul, baffled at first, identified as modern Greek. 'She had mental ebullience and physical exuberance, but she also had tremendous tranquillity. Aphrodite loved laughter, but she didn't laugh much herself, do you think?'

Paul considered this. 'But Mrs Trent was always smiling,' he said. 'I agree you never do see Aphrodite laughing, now I come to think of it. But Mrs Trent smiled all the time.'

Charles said, 'Were you ever alone with her?'

'No. No, I don't think I was, not that I remember.'

'You would remember if you had been. She reflected her company, of course. The men buzzed round her, and she set to her partner instinctively. She was full of light, but the sparkle you saw was mostly reflected.'

'I wonder. You certainly put her in a new light. But then I am perpetually finding myself presented with new pictures of her. I must say, I find it a little difficult to reconcile yours with the quality I was so conscious of. What you called the barrier of doubtful taste just now – that rang a bell at once. I suppose we're over-educated or something.'

'Oh, no, Mr Mycroft.' Charles wrestled with the exasperation of the very young who cannot communicate their vision. 'You were talking of physical attraction. If I had felt physically attracted to Mrs Trent, the doubtful taste would have been on my side. Rather like using the Venus of Melos as a pin-up. Do you see what I mean? I suppose the vulgar-minded could do that. That's why you get north-country city fathers objecting to serious nudes as an affront to public decency.'

'Oh dear.' Paul thought again and shook his head. 'It's no good, Charles. I can't see Mrs Trent as a serious nude. To me she was pure pin-up.'

'Look, Mr Mycroft. I expect a lot of nude models have been cheerful tarts. The Rubens women, for instance. It comes through in the painting, of course. But that doesn't make the painting pin-up stuff.' He smiled suddenly. 'I'm hanged if I know why, now I come to think of it. I expect I'm talking nonsense.' He did not seem to find the experience at all disturbing.

'I'm sure you're not. It's much too interesting to be nonsense. You may be wrong, but that's immaterial. Don't you get a bit bored here at times?'

'Only with Aristotle. I must say, the Mods. syllabus had much the better reading. But the job's full of interest really, or ought to be anyhow. The view from behind the bar, you know – it's a commonplace, isn't it? Everybody being that bit larger than life. And of course, not being a barmaid, I don't get drawn in. Not usually, anyhow.' He smiled suddenly and dazzlingly at Paul. 'For most of them I am the ideal bystander. They don't mistrust me, as they might an ordinary hotel servant, but they are under no obligation to bring me into the conversation. Give them a drink or two, and they go through all the motions. I ought to write a book, I suppose.' He seemed to find the obligation an unattractive one.

Paul said, 'This is our first visit, of course. I gather you have been here before.'

'I've done four spells now, yes. This is my second long vac., and I've done two Easters. They only open this bar in the season, of course. Jim's bar is the permanent one the locals use between-whiles. I can see just the sort of book I ought to write. Social comedy stuff, with a bit of dirt about holiday affairs.' He seemed gloomier than ever. 'I don't think I'm cut out for social comedy. I've got the facts, of course, but I don't find them wildly amusing.'

'You've got tragedy now,' said Paul.

'Mrs Trent? Yes. I don't think Mrs Trent's death is tragic in itself. It's the sort of small natural disaster, like a spoilt summer. There's always tragedy about, of course, but I wouldn't touch most of it.'

'Here?'

'I think so, yes. Mr Dawson is a tragic figure in a grotesque sort of way, don't you think? So for the matter of that is Major Trent. Or they could be. Frustration is always sad. It probably becomes legitimate tragedy only when it finds some sort of end. I suppose that's on the cards now.'

'Precipitated by Mrs Trent's death, which you say is not tragic in itself? I think you ought to write that book, Charles. I must say, it would need a good deal of dramatic tension to make Mr Dawson into a tragic figure for me. He's sad enough, in all conscience. So is Major Trent, I think. I can't say I like him, though.'

'The tension's there, Mr Mycroft. You're not in the hotel, so you wouldn't know. But there really is quite a degree of it. It's been building up ever since Wednesday.'

'Wednesday? But we only found her on Thursday.'

'I know. But the thing cast its shadow before it. I'm not being fey or anything. Major Trent was looking for Mrs Trent on Wednesday, you know. And you've seen Mr Dawson.'

'Dawson? Yes. He's upset about Mrs Trent's death and he's not, to say the least of it, getting much sympathy from his wife.'

'He's drunk,' said Charles. 'He's reached the stage now where you hardly notice it and he doesn't either.'

'That's it, is it? He drank a lot of rum this evening, I know, and I got the impression, after a bit, that it wasn't having much effect. Has he been at it ever since Mrs Trent's death?'

37

Charles said, 'Her death? I can't answer for that, Mr Mycroft. But he's been drinking ever since Wednesday evening.'

Susan had abandoned her sky-blue trousers and was wearing a dark skirt and jersey. Her hair still hung loose, but she had got most of it behind one ear. She looked more sure of herself. She said, 'I'm not late, am I? I'm sorry you've had to wait.'

'No,' said Paul, 'I was much too early. I've been talking to Charles.'

'And to Mr Dawson?'

'Yes, as a matter of fact. Have you seen him?'

She nodded. 'I saw him upstairs. He told me you were here, but I had to change. Their room is next to mine.'

Paul said, 'Will you have a drink before we go? There's still time.'

'Yes, please. Do you mind awfully if I have a gin? I shan't set your house on fire or sleep at my post. But I really could do with it. These walls are too thin.'

She took the drink and held it in front of her. 'I don't know what to say,' she said. 'Would "God bless" do?'

' "God bless" will do admirably,' said Paul.

CHAPTER FIVE

'Thank you, Mr Mycroft,' said the coroner. 'I'm afraid this has been a distressing thing for you and your family when you were here on holiday.'

Paul hesitated and caught the sergeant's eye. To say 'Not at all' would sound callous or worse. He did not wish to appear in public as the father of a family of ghouls. To admit distress seemed somehow inconsiderate to the coroner, who was plainly concerned for the local tourist industry. He said, 'Thank you, sir. We have tried not to let it distress us too much.'

'That's right,' said the coroner. He seemed on the point of adding, 'We hope you will come again next year,' but contented himself with a friendly smile. 'We shall not need to keep you, then, Mr Mycroft.' Paul bowed and withdrew.

The walls were of granite and the woodwork painted dark green. Outside the summer persisted, but the tall windows, obscured below and not too clean above, filtered the sunlight and took the heart out of it. We have come, thought Paul, to sit in inquest on the body of the laughter-loving Aphrodite. In her life she was an inspiration to the young men and an excitement to the old, she was kind to the young women and a pain in the neck to those whose husbands felt younger than they did. In her death she was a threat to the holiday attractions, of which she had herself in her life been a notable example. The sea has reclaimed her – But here the thing broke down. The sea had not claimed Millie. She had been afraid of it, if Susan's version was true, and had taken precautions against it, but it had got her in the end. It had got her and washed the sunlight out of her and then thrown her up again, with one shoe gone and her hair all over the place, to be put on a mortuary slab and identified by the incredulous china-blue pro-ophthalmia of her husband and sat on in a granite hall which excluded the sunlight.

'What it comes to, Major Trent,' said the coroner, 'is that you did not see your wife again after you had both had breakfast that morning?'

'That is so, yes.' Major Trent appeared to be standing to attention, though his hands and feet were not in the regulation positions. He stared straight ahead, and his speech came horizontally from the rigid nape of his neck.

He's on the mat, Paul thought. So in times past he must have stood before his colonel, rigidly submissive, but giving nothing away. The coroner, not being a colonel, clearly found him puzzling. He was a kindly man with some experience of holiday tragedy, who wished to be tactful and sympathetic, but found his advances shattered on the clipped speech and staring eyes.

'You made some enquiries as to her whereabouts?'

'Yes.' He paused. 'That was later.'

'When you became worried?'

To Paul the silence seemed interminable. If there had been a clock he would have heard it ticking, but the clock in the gallery pointed to half-past five and had clearly stopped. I'm imagining this, he thought. No one else seemed to have noticed anything.

'I was worried, yes,' said Major Trent. 'No one had seen her.'

'When was that?'

'Some time in the evening. I suppose about seven.'

This time it was the coroner who paused. He seemed more puzzled than ever. 'You did not actually make any enquiries until about seven in the evening?' he asked. There was a touch of acid in the balm now.

'I was out during the afternoon.'

'Out?'

'Sailing.'

'Ah. You were out sailing during the afternoon, and when you returned and found your wife was not in, you became worried and made enquiries?' He was visibly comforted by what seemed to him a more acceptable state of affairs.

'That's it,' said Major Trent.

'Your wife did not sail, I take it?'

'Oh yes. She was an experienced sailor.'

40

'But she was not sailing that afternoon?'

Major Trent's mouth opened slightly under his clipped moustache. He took a breath. He is not exactly being insolent, thought Paul. He is making it clear that he knows authority when he sees it, but finds it difficult to understand why some people have it.

'I have told you, sir. I did not see my wife after we had breakfasted, and I do not know where she was.'

'No, no,' said the coroner, 'quite so. So you cannot help us at all to understand how your wife came to be in the water?'

'I'm afraid not,' said Major Trent.

'Thank you, Major Trent. I don't think I need trouble you any further. I hope you will allow me to offer you the court's sympathy in this tragedy that has befallen you on your holiday.'

Major Trent bowed and withdrew. The hollow man, thought Paul. I told Mary he was the original hollow man. But there must be something there. No one can really be as hollow as that. The little hollow husband of the dead goddess. Goddesses had had mortal husbands before now, come to think of it, and mostly they had come to a bad end. The goddesses could not, in the nature of things, come to any end at all, though they could suffer unpleasing transformations. The thing went off the rails again. Millie was, by demonstration, not immortal, and he could not think off-hand of anything she could convincingly be translated into. She was dead, and her hollow husband survived. Perhaps he would now gradually fill up again. He wondered if that was it. He had seen it happen before. Something might even now be stirring cautiously behind the staring mask, hope of a sort, the speculative consideration of the possibility of happiness rather than its anticipation.

He wondered suddenly who had had the money. He was less interested in how the marriage had ended than in why it had survived so long. Money might be the answer. The police might have made it their business to find out, but he did not think so. Even if they had, it was unlikely that the sergeant would tell him. And ten to one money had nothing to do with it anyway. There had been some sort of long-settled inertia, as there was in most marriages. A balance had been struck and, however precarious it looked to the outsider, held, until external forces had struck one side away. But the posture had been extreme and the release of energy must be proportionately sharp. Perhaps this was what Charles had meant when he had talked about tragedy arising from the ending of frustration.

'You have no doubt, doctor,' said the coroner, 'that the deceased met her death by drowning?'

'No,' said the doctor, 'no doubt at all.' He was an old doctor, and an old doctor in those parts knew a drowning case when he saw one. He was carrying out, Paul saw, one of his regular seasonal duties. That did not mean that he had been casual in his examination or was mistaken in his conclusion.

'Did you observe anything, doctor, which might suggest how the deceased had got into the water?'

This time the doctor was really thinking. He said, 'I found some slight injuries. There was some bruising on one ankle and slight abrasions on one hand and one forearm. These would not be inconsistent with the deceased's having slipped and fallen into the water – from a rock, say. They do not, of course, amount to any real evidence that she did so.'

'These injuries were received before death?'

'Oh yes, certainly, but they were very recent.'

'Would they be equally consistent with her having fallen

from a boat?'

The doctor was getting a little impatient. He had begun to put on a bit of an act, Paul noticed, where before he had been following an established routine. He put his head slightly on one side and screwed his mouth up as a calculated indication of mental effort.

'I suppose that could be so. If anything the abrasions, such as they were, would seem more likely to be caused by a relatively rough surface, such as a rock, than by the wooden side of a boat. But I do not think it can be more than speculation either way.'

'Quite so. We must not go beyond our evidence. Thank you, doctor.'

Violence dawned on Paul suddenly, not necessarily the violence of man, but the violence of gravity, which, given the chance, could pull you off the face of a cliff and bring you plunging down to the surface of the sea below and from there, as your struggles weakened, pull you down, more slowly but more fatally, out of reach of the air you needed to survive. Millie alive he knew and had seen through the eyes of several different people. Millie dead he had seen with his own eyes (but he had missed the abrasions), and he had watched the effect of her death spread until it had washed him up in this granite hall where the sunlight could not reach and time went unrecorded. About her death he had thought hardly at all. Now he was suddenly overwhelmed with the horror of it, the scream, the struggle (Millie was all alive and would have fought for survival like a cat), the sudden sickening onset of the thing which had always haunted her, but which she could not keep away from. Paul thought what pain it was to drown, especially if you were a laughter-loving goddess out on a date. He shivered violently and looked guiltily at his neighbours. They were listening to the coroner. They

43

had no alternative, the coroner had said. Yes, he thanked them, they had returned the only possible verdict, which would be duly recorded. Paul lifted himself with all the others from the green-painted bench and found himself momentarily unsteady on cramped legs. People blinked in the strong sunlight and looked at each other with a slight sheepishness, as though they had come out of church.

He saw Mr Dawson moving off from the edge of the swelling knot of people outside the door. He walked quickly in an unnaturally straight line, like a mechanical toy. Something or someone, thought Paul, had wound him up and he must walk until the accumulated force that drove him had spent itself, or until the machinery failed to respond. A driven man, not hollow, but full of works, so that after a bit you could anticipate every inevitable movement, and wondered merely what drove it and how long it would go without recharging. Once more he thought of Charles's tragic figure. A driven man could be tragic, but he must be demon-driven into calamitous action, not buzzing quietly on a couple of dry cells into repetitive and predictable commonplaces. Charles was intelligent but very young. He was full of stimulation, as the young should be, but he was not Sir Oracle.

The sergeant took him by the arm. He said, 'I was wondering could I give you a lift out to Pelant, sir, I've got the car here. That's unless you've got your own arrangements made, or are meeting Mrs Mycroft. I see she's not here.'

'Good gracious, no,' said Paul, 'why should she be? Thank you, it's very kind of you. If it's not inconvenient, I'd like a lift to the house.'

' 'Tis not inconvenient at all. I'd like a word with you, as a matter of fact.'

It was a private car, a black saloon of more respectability than dash. The sergeant, Paul felt sure, took his family out in it when off duty. That he was, or had been, a family man was an assumption so inevitable that it did not consciously come to mind. They crawled out of the holiday traffic and through the raw prosperity of the town's edge towards the beginning of the coast road. It was curious that people living among so much natural beauty should have such deplorable taste, but it was a thing Paul had noticed elsewhere. A man whose forbears had for generations built themselves beautiful and brilliantly serviceable granite and slate cottages would, given a dash of modern money, build and live happily in the most abject bungalow of breeze-blocks coated with coloured pebble-dash. The heavy, indestructible slate would be replaced with asbestos tiles and the stone weather-porch with a shallow verandah of cream-painted woodwork. The people were, for all their obvious prosperity, almost completely unspoilt. They remained cheerful, balanced and, even on a cash basis, instinctively hospitable, so that they glowed with a natural warmth among their uncouth visitors. It was simply that, once the discipline of traditional materials had been removed, they revealed a blind spot for external appearances.

'Do you live near Pelynt yourself?' Paul asked.

'That's right, sir. We've got a bungalow on the Carrow road. A nice little place, and 'tis handy for the station.' Paul did not pursue the matter.

'Well,' said the sergeant presently, as the car settled on to the grey switchback of the coast road, 'they couldn't do nothing much else, could they, sir? We don't know any more now how Mrs Trent come to be in the water than we did when you found her. That's the truth. But she wasn't one to drown herself by all accounts, and I can't see that anyone else wanted her out of the way.'

He stopped on an upward inflection, and Paul knew this

was his cue if he wanted to come in on it. He thought, as no doubt the sergeant was thinking, of Major Trent's uncharacteristic enquiries. He thought of a salt-stained lifejacket at the bottom of a cupboard and Mr Dawson's sudden recourse to rum. But really there was nothing, nothing at all, except the speculations of Charles when his mind wandered from his Aristotle. And Charles had seen Millie as a creature of warmth and tranquillity and her death as a minor natural disaster. Like a spoilt summer, he had said. An excellent phrase, only to Paul it still did not really make sense. He shook his head.

'Not that I know of,' he said.

'Of course,' said the sergeant, 'someone knows more than they're admitting. Mrs Trent was going to meet someone, I still think, and we don't know who. But that's not saying they pushed her in the sea, or that anyone did, for that matter. You heard what the doctor said about her slipping. We've only found one chap who was out Bartenny way that afternoon, a young chap called Cardew, a fisherman. But he saw nothing. And of course he had his work to do out there.'

'Cardew? I think I've heard the name. He does a bit of hiring or something, doesn't he? Trips round the Tabernacles if the weather's good enough or a bit of off-shore fishing for those that want it – that sort of thing.'

'Sure to. Or if he doesn't, he's the only one. There's more ways of making money with a boat than by fishing and picking up lobsters. But he's a nice young chap, not much to him. If he says he saw nothing, he didn't. And anyway, what was there to see, when you come to think? Mrs Trent going along the cliff, now, in that pale blue jersey – you'd see her all right from the sea. 'Tis wonderful the way figures show up on the cliffs from a boat, as you've no doubt seen for yourself. And of course, if you happened to look at just the right moment, you'd see them fall in if they went in. But a head in the water's different. That's the danger of going overboard in anything but a flat calm. They'll come round and look for you, and you may see them, but even when they're looking it's odds on they won't see you till they're right on top of you. And if nobody's looking for you, you could swim all day without being seen. From a boat, that is. There again, from the cliff you'd be seen all right, but there's not many up there, and the coastguards can't be everywhere. No, there's no reason why anyone should have seen her, and from the looks of it no one did. Her only chance was to get out for herself, and that's not always easy.'

In the warmth of the closed car Paul shivered again. He had been over all this back in the granite hall, and it did not help to have the details of his imagining filled in, even in the warm businesslike voice of the sergeant. He nodded but said nothing. The sergeant said unexpectedly, ' 'Tis nasty, I know, sir, especially when it was you found her and you knew the lady. People don't think enough how it is, that's the truth. They're all alive and playing with the sea one minute, and the next one of them's dead and the rest think it sad and are glad it wasn't them. But they don't think how it happened, nor what it felt like while it was happening. Well there, probably they'll never know, and why upset themselves? But I sometimes think if they did, they'd be more careful. But don't you go letting your mind dwell on it, sir. I can see it's worrying you a bit. I shouldn't think no more about it. I reckon that's the last we'll hear of Mrs Trent, or of the Major either, I'd say. He'll be off away from here this afternoon, he tells me, and I don't suppose he'll be back.'

Paul nodded. He said, 'Thank you, sergeant. I'm sorry you had to give me a pep-talk. But you're perfectly right.

47

I did get the horrors a bit for the moment. There have been too many people talking and I've been letting my mind dwell on it. And as you say, you don't imagine the thing happening, and then suddenly it hits you. We may take it that the case is closed, may we?'

The sergeant said nothing for a minute. Then he said, 'Well, as to that, sir, the coroner's verdict don't settle nothing. So long as we don't know what happened, I expect we'll remain curious. That's our job. But I don't see myself how our curiosity's going to be satisfied. If this will do you, sir, I'll put you off at the top of the road here. 'Tis but a step down to your house.'

'Yes. That will do fine. Thank you very much for the lift.' He raised his hand in salute and the black car moved off.

As he crossed the pebbles, Susan shot out of the verandah. She looked at him with an odd mixture of exasperation and apology. 'Mummy's here,' she said.

'Ah,' said Paul, 'Good morning, Mrs Frayne.'

CHAPTER SIX

'Good morning,' said Mrs Frayne. 'You've got back awfully quickly.' She spoke upwards in a little thin voice, as though from a chronic bed of pain. She sat perfectly relaxed in the most comfortable of the verandah chairs and had a glass at her elbow. Her feet were tiny.

'Oh yes,' said Paul. 'It didn't take long. And the sergeant gave me a lift home as he was coming this way.'

'The sergeant?' She seemed to have heard of sergeants, but could form no very clear picture of what they looked like.

48

'A policeman,' said Paul, 'with three stripes on his arm.'

'Oh, a policeman.' She shrank in on herself and made no further comment.

'Have they finished?' said Mary, 'or did you come away when you'd got through your bit?' She looked at him with a twinge of anxiety. 'Here, get this down. You look a bit worn at the edges.' Mrs Frayne raised her head and looked at him curiously. She was interested in physical symptoms. His edges seemed perfectly smooth, and she lay back.

'Thanks. I do rather need it. Oh yes, they've finished. It didn't take long. What I believe is called an open verdict. They couldn't do anything else, I imagine. Millie Trent was drowned, not poisoned or bashed on the head. That's just about all anybody knows. Or were you expecting an early arrest?'

'Arrest?' said Mrs Frayne. 'Why should anyone be arrested?'

There was a pause. Then Susan said, 'For murdering Mrs Trent.' Her voice was unexpectedly loud and harsh. She was looking fixedly at her mother.

'But did anybody murder her?'

'No, that's the whole point. And Mrs Mycroft wasn't really expecting an arrest. But if she had been, the arrest would have been for the murder of Mrs Trent. Only there won't be an arrest because no one murdered her.'

Mrs Frayne shut her eyes and frowned slightly. 'I can't think why,' she said. 'Don't talk quite so loud, Susan darling. I've got a shocking head.'

'Mummy—' Susan broke off, the usually sulky underlip standing out alarmingly.

A confused clamour came from inside the house, followed by the sound of breaking crockery. 'Children eating already?' said Paul.

Mary nodded. 'I gave them their lunch early.'

'One more off the inventory, anyway,' said Paul. He pulled out a pocket diary and made a note. 'One plate,' he said. 'That's the third in two days.'

'Sounded more like a cup,' said Mary.

'Cups at lunch?'

'Cheaper than glasses.'

'I'll see to it,' said Susan. She went indoors.

Mrs Frayne said, 'It's so good of you to take pity on Susan. She gets so bored, you know, and then she gets difficult. Her father and I don't find it at all easy.'

'Where is Colonel Frayne?' said Mary.

'Oh, he's out sailing. In the boat. The Watson child is helping him. It's a pity Susan doesn't go out more, but she's not very clever in the boat, and he says it makes such a difference having someone who is. I don't think Susan wants to much, but it would make something for her to do. And of course, I can't do much for her.' She sighed comfortably.

'We're not taking pity on her, you know,' said Paul. 'She is on us. She is worth her weight in gold with the family. I don't think Mary really started her holiday until Susan began to lend a hand.'

Mrs Frayne gave a gentle, deprecating little laugh. 'Poor Sue,' she said, 'I'm afraid she's not really much good about the house, but it's very kind of you to be so nice about her.' She wrinkled an unmarked forehead. 'She used to talk to Mrs Trent quite a lot, you know. Her father and I didn't like it, but it's difficult when people are staying in the same hotel. I must say, I'm glad that's over.'

Paul looked at her incredulously. He said, 'You mean—' but Mary cut him short.

'I think, as you say, she was bored,' she said, 'and found Mrs Trent cheerful company.'

'Cheerful?' Mrs Frayne's voice achieved a miniature shriek. 'Well, really – I suppose if you find vulgarity pleasant, you might have found her good company. And of course, so far as the men were concerned she was sure to be a success, or at any rate with any man who wasn't too particular. Henry says she laid herself out to please, but that's rather naughty of him.' She gave a tinkling laugh and then caught her breath as if it had hurt her. 'Henry could be very funny about her, I must say.' She stretched out one of her hands and examined it minutely, as if to assure herself of the particularity of Henry's taste.

'I hope he won't stop being funny about her just because she's dead,' said Paul. 'That would be a pity. But from all other points of view you must be glad she's out of the way.'

Mary said, 'Paul—' but Mrs Frayne said, 'Well, of course it is a relief. Not that, apart from Susan, she ever did me any particular harm. Poor Agnes Dawson, now – it must be a real relief to her.' She sighed and shut her eyes. Then she opened them and said, 'But of course, I don't expect she had anything to do with it.'

Paul said, 'Do with it? Oh, I see. Surely, Mrs Frayne, if every wife whose husband looked at Mrs Trent with eyes on stalks' – he could not be sure whether to be glad or sorry that Susan had gone inside – 'had tried to murder her, she'd have died years ago, if from nothing else, from sheer weight of numbers. And in any case I can't really see Mrs Dawson and Mrs Trent locked in combat on the water's edge over Agnes's Jack, however much of a grievance Agnes may have felt she had.'

Mrs Frayne shut her eyes again. The china-clay brow wrinkled and she made a little moaning sound. 'Apart from which,' said Paul, taking no notice, 'if Agnes had pushed Millie in, I can't see why Millie couldn't simply have climbed out again.'

Mrs Frayne opened her eyes and stared at him. 'But the boat would have gone on again,' she said.

'Who talked of a boat? For what it's worth, Mrs Dawson never goes in a boat.'

'But I said Agnes had nothing to do with it.' The tiny, high-pitched voice faltered, and she looked stricken.

'And again for what it's worth,' said Paul, 'the doctor who gave evidence this morning thought she might have slipped off a rock, but not off a boat.'

'Then why didn't she climb out again?'

Mary snorted discreetly, and Paul felt suddenly silly. He said, 'Nobody knows what happened, Mrs Frayne. Mrs Trent was drowned, but nobody knows how.'

Mrs Frayne smiled. 'Somebody knows all right,' she said. 'What nobody knows is who that somebody is.'

Paul said, 'Oh lor.'

Susan appeared and said, 'Mummy, it's time we started walking back to the hotel.'

Mary said, 'Oh hullo, Major Trent. How very kind of you to come and see us.' Mrs Frayne sat up with a sudden-ness that did credit to her muscular reflexes.

'Just looked in to say good-bye,' said Major Trent. 'I'm going home this afternoon.'

'That's very nice of you,' said Paul. 'You shouldn't have bothered. But now you're here, you're going to sit down and have a drink.'

Major Trent blinked at the surrounding faces. 'No, really,' he said. 'I didn't know you'd got company, or I shouldn't have bothered you. You must have got back very quickly, Mycroft.'

'Please don't mind me,' said Mrs Frayne. She uncoiled herself and stood up with the minimum of apparent effort and, Paul grudgingly admitted to himself, very real grace. 'We're just going anyhow. We've got to get back to the

Carrack, and I don't walk very fast, you know.'

Susan walked suddenly across her mother and stood squarely in front of Major Trent. Head up and shoulders back, she was as tall as he was. She held out her hand. 'Major Trent,' she said, 'I haven't seen you since your wife's death. I just wanted to say how terribly sorry I am. It – it was a horrible blow to me, you know. I can't think what it must be to you.'

His eyes opened suddenly into almost perfect circles and then hooded themselves. He took her hand, and Paul noticed that when his pudgy hand spread itself it was extremely muscular. He had the impression that for the moment they were completely unaware of anyone else's existence. Major Trent said, 'That's very kind of you, Susan. Millie was very fond of you, of course. She always had her friends.'

Paul said, 'She had a great many. Even at Pelant.'

Susan turned to Mary. 'I'll come this evening, shall I?' she said.

'I wish you would. But not if you've got anything better to do. We don't want to be a burden to you.'

'No burden,' said Susan. 'I love it here.' She set off down the path, still holding herself very straight. Mrs Frayne, without apparently setting herself in motion, contrived to be, if not beside her, at least with her. She said, 'Yes, we must be going. Good-bye, Mary. Good-bye Major Trent.' They crunched off over the pebbles. Susan had not turned round.

Major Trent looked from Paul to Mary. His eyes were still hooded, but his mouth held the suggestion of a smile. He said, 'I hope I have not interrupted your conversation.'

'You have,' said Paul. 'We are indebted to you. It is difficult to be comfortable with both Susan and her mother.'

Major Trent nodded. 'Nice girl, that,' he said. 'Frayne must find it difficult.'

'He seems to manage to enjoy himself,' said Paul.

Major Trent took the drink handed to him and stroked down his moustache. 'You think so? I suppose he gets what amusement he can. Keen on sailing, of course. I mean really keen. I often wonder how many of them enjoy it as much as they say they do. Especially the women. The discomfort, you know, and the weather and the comic rig-out. All right for the very young, who think they look beautiful in anything. And of course you get the mothers who feel it's worth tagging along just to keep their grip on the family. But half the women go out because a man takes them out, and most of the other half go out to make sure the man doesn't take anybody else. And half of them are scared half the time if it's blowing a bit.'

Paul said, 'Your wife was an expert, I gather.'

'She enjoyed it, yes.' He put his glass down and turned round to look at Paul. 'However she came to be in the sea,' he said, 'she didn't go in off a boat.' He spoke very deliberately. 'I could have told the coroner that without the doctor's evidence.'

'You don't sail yourself much?'

'I like it occasionally, but I won't make a thing of it. Don't care for racing. Like going out single-handed, as a matter of fact, if the weather's right. It's nice being out on the sea alone.' He said it as if he was talking to himself. Then he recovered himself and said, almost apologetically, 'You really are alone, though, aren't you, in a boat? Good thing, occasionally.' He looked into his glass, found he still had something left in it, looked quickly from one to the other of them and went on, as if by compulsion, talking. 'Still,' he said, 'I shan't be here next year, of course. Got to think what I want to do, as a matter of fact. Things will be very different now.'

Paul thought of the invisibly divided bedroom, with the Major's neat and meagre requirements ranged on the chest-of-drawers. By himself, he thought, he would need only a very small room, and then he would never really fill it. The habit of self-contraction had become too ingrained. 'I'm afraid I don't know where you live,' he said.

'Tonbridge. Not a big place, of course, but getting crowded like everywhere else. I've been thinking of Scotland, as a matter of fact – the west coast. Still, there are a lot of things to settle first.'

He finished his drink and rose. 'I must be getting on. Good-bye, Mrs Mycroft. Thank you again for what you did. We shan't meet again, I imagine.' He said this to Paul.

'I'll come to the gate,' said Paul. The major said nothing, and they walked down the pebbled path in silence. Then he stopped and held out his hand. 'Good-bye, Mycroft,' he said.

'Good-bye,' said Paul. They shook hands with a curious solemnity. Major Trent set off down the rough road between the tamarisks. Then he hesitated and turned. 'I meant to say,' he said, 'I'm afraid I never found your wife's scarf.'

'No?' said Paul. 'It doesn't matter in the least. I don't think she's thought of it.'

'No? No, exactly.' He turned and marched off.

Paul went back into the verandah. His wife was inside the house doing what they called settling the children. The after-lunch settlement was a relic of the siesta of their younger days, jealously preserved as an instrument of sanity and good temper. He hesitated and then, as an unaccustomed indulgence, re-filled his glass. He found himself absorbed by the picture of Major Trent, who could hardly fill a small room, trying in a small boat to fill the

empty waste of sea. He wondered what the uncommunica-
tive mask would look like in so great a solitude. He tried
to imagine the major singing to himself but could not
manage it. He would sit there, watching the movements
of water and wind and responding to them, through tiller
and sheet, with those unexpectedly muscular and purposive
hands. He would be absorbed and quiescent. And happy,
thought Paul. So far as he could associate a positive
happiness with Major Trent, it would come with solitude
and quiescence. Hence, he supposed, the west coast of
Scotland. A curious man.

'If someone would only drown Mrs Frayne,' said Mary,
'I would go and pour an extra bucketful of water over her
myself to make assurance doubly sure. But what do you
think of Susan? She's unexpected, that girl, isn't she? One
of these days the Fraynes are in for a shock with their
Susan.'

'It's Frayne that will get the shock. Mrs Frayne, dear
fragile little Mrs Frayne, knows what she's up against all
right. That sort of woman always does. Her father
probably thinks she's just a nice kid and devoted to him.
In his way he's the worse of the two. But not deliberately
wicked, like his wife. But she'll never get near enough the
water for anyone to drown her. You'll have to think of
something else. Anyway, drowning's too good for her. She
wants to be made to work out her punishment. I mean
work, do you see? She ought to have everything cut
suddenly from under her and have to work out her salvation in conditions of intolerable severity and squalor.'

'The odd thing is,' said Mary, 'that she'd survive. She's
as tough as they come, physically as well as mentally, and
she is constitutionally in a miraculous state of preservation.
Well, there's nothing miraculous about it really. She's
concentrated on self-preservation from the time she was

born. She'll outlive us all, through long years of decorative and cushioned widowhood.'

'I'm afraid she will. No one's really going to get back at her. Nasty as she undoubtedly is, she doesn't draw people's fire in the way Millie did, or even Mrs Dawson. That sort of complete egotism has its safeguards, so long as it is in a position to indulge itself. It is simply not sufficiently interested in other people to injure them deliberately. I don't imagine for a moment she gives Frayne hell, of the kind old Leatherlegs gets from Agnes. He's probably quite fond of her in a way, and certainly rather proud of her. He really believes in her sufferings, and she doesn't tie him nearly as close as Agnes ties her Jack. Even with the child her evil is a sort of negative evil. Susan's survived, you see. In fact, she's done a good deal better than that. She probably had plenty of affection from her father in his way, and she probably loved him well enough until her critical powers developed. And by then she was safe. She's too much contempt for her mother to allow her to crush her. And as I said just now, Mrs Frayne knows that perfectly well, and will play safe. Given some really direct head-on clash of interest, there might be trouble. But when Susan decides to become a Communist or a missionary or marry an Indonesian, her mother will simply wash her hands of her. As I said, it's her father that will get the shock.'

They sat for a minute in silence, while the tamarisks rustled in the breeze that came up from Lanting. Then Mary said, 'Do you know, I still like Major Trent. I can't make head or tail of him, but I don't think he's as hollow as you think. There is something there I like.'

'I think I know what you mean. But I think he's changed quite a bit, or at any rate is changing. I think he's filling up.'

'Since Millie's death?'

'I think so, yes.'

Mary said, 'It doesn't say much for matrimony, does it?' Her voice was slightly hollow, and Paul smiled at her.

'It was a pretty odd sort of matrimony, you know. I don't feel a bit hollow.'

'Well that's something. If I die and you start filling up, I'll come back at night and hollow you out again.'

Paul looked at her with alarm. 'The vampire,' he said, 'the succubus. The avenging female horror. Why are women so fierce about things?'

They held hands. Mary said, 'Only some things. But Major Trent is a puzzle, isn't he? One keeps on nearly pinning him down and then he's gone again. What was he like this morning?'

'What you'd imagine. Sort of actively negative. Giving nothing away. If it's any comfort to you, he puzzled the poor little coroner as much as he puzzles you. He doesn't ask for sympathy much, does he?'

'Not at all. I don't even know why he came here today. He presumably came to talk, but he seemed disconcerted to find anyone here.'

Paul smiled. 'I know why he came,' he said.

CHAPTER SEVEN

As it got nearer the sea, the family, which had set out as a recognisable social group, straggled more and more. Cathleen, with a characteristic dancing step, took the lead. She held the youngest sister in ·one hand and the assorted gear of both in the other. How Julia kept pace with Cathleen was a thing their parents had never determined. She seemed at times to be half flying, like Alice in the grip of the Red Queen. She did not mind in the least.

Jennifer came by herself, some way behind, walking reflectively. She carried her own gear, nicely calculated and carefully collected, and nothing else whatsoever. Paul and Mary came at a longer interval but never quite out of touch. Paul carried most of the baggage and Mary, with her eyes on the children, most of the responsibility. As they came out over the dunes, the river opened up in front of them, bright blue, with the heavy internal sheen of lead crystal. Paul said, 'Thank God the weather's right.'

'It's perfect. Anyhow, I imagine the boat's pretty stable, isn't it? Not like a racing dinghy, I mean?'

'Not in the least like a racing dinghy. Clinker-built with solid planking and a solid engine properly housed in board. And you steer it with a wheel. It's a working boat, after all.'

'I was thinking of Susan, as a matter of fact. The children wouldn't mind what the boat did until the water started coming in in bulk. But you said Susan wasn't really happy in a boat.'

'A crypto-hydrophobe, by her own account,' said Paul. 'But pretty crypto. She only doesn't like hanging out over the side in sheets of spray with the lee gunwale half under. I'm not at all sure I blame her. That sort of thing is for the enthusiast. If the lee gunwale of Cardew's boat gets half under, we're really in trouble. But on a day like this we might as well be on the Queen Mary. In fact, we're a lot safer than on the Queen Mary. Not nearly so far to fall. There's Susan now.'

Cathleen had also seen Susan, and Julia's feet were now perceptibly clear of the ground for long intervals. Mary said, 'Golly, is that Cardew?'

'That's him and that's the boat. Why?'

'Why?' said Mary. 'Haven't you got eyes? He's too

59

wonderful to be true.'

'Is he? It hadn't struck me quite so forcibly, but then I'm the wrong sex. Young, sunburnt, picturesque. Chiefly young – the sort that makes me feel suddenly middle-aged. I hadn't realised he was the answer to a maiden's prayer.'

'Maiden my foot,' said Mary. 'Lead me to him.'

Susan was in trousers, but they were black and not too tight. Her jersey was the darkest possible red, high-necked, and her lank dark hair gathered behind her head. 'She's growing up,' thought Paul with a sudden twinge of new interest. If Mary could have her excitements, so could he.

The white boat, heavily fendered, lay motionless against the granite steps. She carried her official number on the bows for all to see. If she had a name, it was discreetly tucked away on the transom, and would be something traditional, not fancy. By the time they reached the jetty the rest of the party had introduced themselves and the children were doing most of the talking.

Mary said, 'Good afternoon, Mr Cardew. We've got a wonderful day, haven't we?' It was curious, thought Paul, how differently even the properest woman will speak to the right sort of man. The time had been, and occasionally still was, when they would do it to him. Mary was no Millie, nor was she kittenish, or eager, or coy. It was mostly the tone of voice and the way the eyes went with the words. He liked to hear it, but couldn't be bothered to work out whether this was a virtue in him or not.

'Good afternoon,' said Cardew. 'You're certainly lucky in your weather. There'll be more of a breeze outside, but not more than's comfortable.' He spoke, for their benefit, a modified, deliberate speech that was neither purely local nor artificially refined. It was rather like a considerate man talking his own language carefully for the benefit of a foreigner not fully at home in it. The effect was very pleasant. He did not call Paul sir, but did not speak to him as an equal. His manner towards Mary was an automatic response, which Paul immediately recognised, to her manner towards him, not familiar, but direct, smiling and with the faintest suggestion of challenge. He dealt with the children with the accustomed ease of an elder brother. To Susan he spoke hardly at all. They said only what needed to be said and that in the simplest possible terms. He had no conversation. The sergeant had called him a nice young chap with nothing much to him. On the first count Paul agreed: he liked Cardew very much. On the second he was inclined to reserve judgment. The afternoon promised well.

They stowed the baggage and distributed the children in the bows, and Susan, her hair blowing back as the boat moved off, stood with them facing straight ahead. Paul and Mary sat one on each side and the fisherman took the wheel. The sun struck up off the sandy bottom through zircon-coloured water. The engine beat with a pleasant subdued thud and the exhaust, unlike the clinging blue miasma of the outboard, went discreetly away astern. The river mouth unfolded round them. The jetty they had just left, with the houses and hotel behind it, seemed already remote. They were off.

The sand dunes on their right rose into a green domed hill and fell away into the flat golden stretch of Lanting Bay. On their left the wooded slopes broke down into successive small inlets and then dropped back like the sides of an amphitheatre round the blue horsehoe of Skittle Cove. Only Skittle Hill, bracken patched and topped with its seamark, stood between them and the veritable Atlantic. On the other side, still stretching away ahead of them, the huge humped mass of Bartenny Head leaned breathlessly on the level sea.

The breeze freshened imperceptibly but put no barrier between their skins and the tremendous radiation of the afternoon sun. Cardew eased up the throttle and the note of the engine rose. The water, deep green now and bottomless, slid past at a quicker pace. Skittle Hill fell back suddenly, and as they crept towards Bartenny the huge vista of shimmering headlands grew up out of the heat haze on either hand. The river was all behind them now. They were at sea.

A long flat sea-swell, hardly visible except in the eye of the sun, lifted the boat and, seconds later, put her down again with the gentleness of superabundant strength. The thudding of the engine sank gradually below the level of their consciousness and became only a foil for the movement of air in the tremendous silence.

The fisherman said, 'There's handlines up under the foredeck, if they'd like to put them out. You never know but what we might pick up a mackerel.' He spoke, apparently, to the nape of Susan's neck under its blown-back cloud of hair.

She did not turn or speak, but stooped at once to where the lines were stowed and, bringing them out, helped first Cathleen and then Jennifer to pay them out clear of the sides of the boat. Paul wondered whether she had handled spinners before. They were the stock-in-trade of the off-shore potterer, not of the dinghy racing enthusiast. Of course they were simple enough; but surely there was no mistaking the tentative movements of hands that worked even the simplest apparatus for the first time. The two little girls, the reels on the floorboards behind them and the lines looped round expectant fingers, were utterly absorbed. Julia, with almost equal absorption, waited to see what would happen. Susan went back to her watch, standing motionless and staring straight ahead. No mackerel came to hand.

A gull wheeled across them and Paul, following its flight over his shoulder, found the cliffs of Bartenny filling the sky behind him. Higher and higher, as they crept under them, the black vertical masses hung between the green slopes above and the blue levels below. Only here and there an evanescent gleam of white showed where the sea worked on the tumbled debris at their foot. For the rest the swell, just audible now but with no motion that the eye could catch, ground stealthily at the tremendous bastion of rock.

Ahead of them the outline swelled at its base, split to let in an unexpected wedge of sky and then, as the boat came further round, threw off part of itself in a splintered cone of black rock topped with green beyond a level stretch of sea. Cathleen took her eyes off her trailing line and pointed ecstatically with her free hand. 'The Tabernacles,' she said.

'Are we going round them?' Paul asked.

'Go anywhere today,' said Cardew.

'I'd like to go between them and the head. I've often wanted to but never had the weather – or the boat.'

Cardew nodded. 'I'll take her through,' he said.

Jennifer said suddenly, 'What does a fish feel like?' There was an almost religious awe in her voice.

'Jerks,' said Cardew, 'instead of a steady pull.'

Susan leant over and took Jennifer's line between finger and thumb. 'Pull it in,' she said. 'No need to wind the line on the reel, but don't get it tangled. Let it fall on the floor boards behind you, and leave it exactly as it falls.' Jennifer, breathing heavily through her nose, pulled in hand over hand, till a glittering flash showed momentarily in the oily wake of the boat. 'You've got one,' said Cardew. 'Pull him in careful. I'll get the hook out.'

From across the boat Mary said, 'It would be Jennifer.'

'It's the concentration,' said Paul. 'Goes right down the line. The fish can't help themselves. You wait till she starts on the men.'

'Poor fish,' said Mary.

There was a wet flurry and excited cries up in the bows, and the beautiful thing came aboard. Cathleen, just old enough to cope with the injustice of fishes, hung on to her own line and watched over her shoulder. Julia clustered round Jennifer. Susan stooped over them. Then she said, 'Put the spinners out again, Jennifer, and let the line go with them. Carefully. If it gets tangled stop it at once.' She turned and, straight between Mary and Paul, threw the fish back to Cardew, who caught it, did something sharp to it with a brown right hand and dropped it behind him in the stern sheets. Jennifer got her line out again and Susan resumed her watch. The boat moved in steadily under the black rock.

High above them a tangle of green paths criss-crossed the broken slopes. Nothing moved on them, but Paul saw with his mind's eye a small figure, parti-coloured in two shades of blue, climbing eagerly while the last grains of sand ran out through the waist of the glass. Lord, lord, he thought, what a fearful way to fall. Then he thought, but it can't have been like that. She'd have been broken up. From much less height than this even a skilled diver can break his back if he gets his angle wrong. A struggling woman, even going direct into the sea, would have looked as if an express train had hit her. It can't have been that.

He turned round. Cathleen and Jennifer, intent on their lines, had not moved. Mary and Julia, heads back and jaws slightly dropped, gazed up at the heights above them. He had never realised how exactly they were alike, and could not understand, even now, why it should move him so.

The engine put on more speed. The boat vibrated, and the water came with a smooth rush along her sides. Very slowly, almost, it seemed, inch by inch, the rocks closed in on both sides of them. The Tabernacles were half the height of the head, but from the sea they were impressive enough. The primeval awe of Scylla and Charybdis took hold of him as the boat fought her way through.

' 'Tis the tide-run,' Cardew said. 'Comes through this way very fast at the half-ebb and back at the half-flood.'

Paul said, a little breathlessly, 'It must be bad if the wind's against it.'

The fisherman, his eyes steady on the vibrating bows, said, ' 'Tis murder,' and Paul's mind, already sensitized by its surroundings, took the word like a blow under the ribs. They were a long way, here, from the Carrack and the playful poison of Mrs Frayne. They were a long way, even, from the world of coloured shorts and the varnished topsides of racing dinghies. Hotel and club gossip could say anything, but out here, in the tide run between Bartenny and the Tabernacles, anything could happen.

The rocks fell back suddenly. The thud of the engine died down and the boat went forward smoothly into an almost windless expanse of bright blue water. Jennifer, without a word, began pulling in her line again. She did it exactly as Susan had showed her. Then Cathleen said, 'I think—' and turned to Susan for help.

From the stern the fisherman spoke with something like professional interest in his voice. 'If you've got two on now, you'll get more,' he said. 'Get them in quick as you can. I'll keep the boat round for a bit.' He began to turn in a wide slow circle, clear of the trailing lines.

The next few minutes were magical and chaotic. Cathleen even at one point found fish on both spinners of her line. Julia screamed and the other two fished incredulously but steadily. The only time Paul saw Susan's face was when she turned to throw the fish back to Cardew. It was grave, absorbed and slightly flushed. None of the children showed any qualms over their flapping victims. He was glad of this, not because he wanted them insensitive, but because he did not want their enjoyment spoilt or, selfishly, his own peace disturbed by the need to deal with unhappiness elsewhere. With the fish once caught and no one, except the fish, the worse, the afternoon was theirs for all time. The sun, the blue water and black rocks, would be part of the picture, over-printed, with any luck, by similar pictures of other summers. It was the fishing they would remember; and the fish might not come quite like this ever again.

As suddenly as it had begun the excitement was over. For a minute nothing happened. The boat nosed round in its wide circle, but no fish came. Their failure to appear was at first as incredible as their original appearance had been, but the balance of probability re-asserted itself.

'We've lost them,' Cardew said at last. 'I reckon they've gone in by the rocks. But we took a dozen nice ones while we had them.'

Paul said, 'Shall we wind in now and have tea?'

'May as well. There'll only be the odd one now.'

The children, glutted with success and hungry with the excitement, were ready for food. The lines were wound in and stowed. They dug out the tea baskets and brought them aft; and Susan at last turned and came back down the boat.

What breeze there had been had died out, and with all Bartenny Bay before them the fisherman stood easily to his wheel. The apprehension of a social problem threw a shadow over Mary's mind. She counted the cups they had brought in the baskets and could not make them, even including the top of the flask, come to more than six. She looked uncertainly at Paul and found him watching Susan.

Susan, her legs tucked neatly under her in the bottom of the boat, looked up at Cardew. He may, Mary thought, have dropped his eyes for a moment, but his head did not move. He said, 'In the bag under the thwart there, do you mind?'

Susan leant forward and pulled out the haversack. She took out flask and cup, poured out and handed it up to him. He nodded, his eyes still ahead. 'Thanks very much,' he said. Mary caught Paul's eye and went back to her tea making.

The children ate and ate and the afternoon wore on. Paul lit a pipe and left the smoke hanging above the glassy water as the way of the boat carried them clear of it. He had never seen such a calm. The sun lost its bite and dropped towards the vast black outline of Bartenny Head. Cardew turned the boat's head out to sea and gave the engine more throttle. Suddenly, but quite decisively, the afternoon was over and they were going home. The blue and silver fish lay limp and salt smelling in the cool under the stern sheets. The children hung their heads over the side, stupefied with food and air and the sun's reflection in their faces. Never for a moment, thought Paul, had perfection wavered. It happened sometimes; he knew it could happen. But he was aware of an apprehension.

In the first yellow of the evening the boat crept up a shrunken river and put her nose gently on the edge of the sand that lay between them and the jetty. They got ashore, the children with much hauling and excitement, Mary handed in state from the fisherman to her husband, Susan without help or fuss. The children clutched a mackerel each, slippery but indubitably theirs. Mary had three, wrapped, in the bottom of a basket. 'The rest are yours,' said Paul.

'Well,' said Cardew. He selected two with inscrutable deliberation, threaded them neatly through the gills on a piece of string and held them out to Susan.

'You can use them?' he said.

For the first time that afternoon she seemed taken aback. 'I don't know,' she said. 'Perhaps they'd cook them for me. Thank you.' She took the fish and gave him a quick sidelong smile.

Paul said, 'I'll come and settle our debt tomorrow.'

'That's all right, There's no hurry.'

Everybody thanked everybody. It was all rather solemn. Even on the children the miracle of the afternoon lay a little heavily. Cardew put his engine into reverse, raised his hand in salute and backed the boat off into what was left of the river.

'Bed,' said Mary to the children, 'if you can stay awake that long. And mackerel for breakfast.'

'Thank you,' said Susan. 'It was perfect.'

'I know,' said Paul, 'almost too perfect. I hope we have deserved it.'

She said perfectly seriously, 'I think it will be all right.' She went off over the sand, dangling her silver fish on their string. The family set their faces to the dunes.

'He's nice,' said Mary. 'Nicer than you'd expect with those looks.'

'I wonder if Susan will manage to eat her fish.'

Mary laughed, with the faintest wobble in it. 'I suppose so. If I were her age, I'd sleep with them under my pillow.'

Paul slung the baskets and the already semi-conscious Julia over his shoulder and they made for the house.

CHAPTER EIGHT

'Of course, Bannerman,' said Dawson's voice, 'to me you're just a bloody mystery.' He laughed heartily as Paul came in. 'Hullo, Mycroft,' he said. 'I was just saying to this chap, to me he's a bloody mystery. He lives all the year round right alongside the sea and the river, and he never leaves the land. Hasn't even got a boat. There's poor sods like me living in the suburbs who come all the way down here once a year for a few weeks' sailing, and this so-and-so lives here all the time and isn't even interested. It beats me.'

'I'm a farmer,' said Bannerman. He nodded to Paul. 'We haven't met,' he said.

'No?' said Dawson. 'Sorry and all that. This is Paul Mycroft, who is staying in a house above Lanting with his charming wife and family. Paul, this is Bannerman, who farms in a big way in these parts and never goes to sea. A bloody mystery, I call him.' He laughed again.

Bannerman smiled at Paul. His face had a bone-deep all-the-year-round tan that made Dawson's seasonal gloss look slightly spurious. 'Charles, give Mr Mycroft whatever he fancies. As I say, I'm a farmer. My interests extend to as near the water as I can get anything to grow. In most places that's the top of the cliff. The sea is a very effective boundary fence, that's all. Of course, nothing's private below high-water mark, but as in most of the places I'm interested in the distance between high and low water is strictly vertical, that doesn't bother me. But you know, most of the chaps who work for me never go near the sea. Apart from anything else, they've got work to do. Their kids swim, of course.'

Paul said to Dawson, 'There's no mystery really, you know. It's always been so. The farmer turned his back on the sea and built his house, if he could manage it, where he couldn't see it. The chaps who went to sea, the fishermen and the seamen, were always a race apart. And anyway, give a seaman a bit of money, and the first thing he'd do was buy a bit of land and build a house in a valley, where all he could see was trees. It's the townsman who feels the sea in his blood. Most of the country's seamen come from places like Sheffield. And in point of fact, after a year or two at sea, most of them go back there. You and I aren't interested in the sea. We're just taking the waters. There's no reason why Bannerman should take them just because he lives handy to them.'

Bannerman smiled and Dawson said nothing. Bannerman had very white, evenly set teeth under a clipped grey moustache. It was funny, thought Paul, that this determined farmer should be everybody's idea of the retired officer.

Dawson was in no mood to meet rational argument. He stared at Paul blankly and shrugged. 'Well, all I can say is, it beats me.' He waved his glass. 'God speed the plough.' he said.

Bannerman said to Paul, 'You're here on holiday, I take it?'

'I'm a tripper,' said Paul. 'We don't even sail, not seriously. We took a house rather than stay somewhere because with a young family it really is easier. But we just bathe and moon about and eat cream teas. We even go for trips round the Tabernacles in hired motor boats. Personally, I enjoy every minute of it, given the weather.'

'I don't blame you. My idea of a holiday, of course, is a solid week of theatres and concerts in London. I do it when I can find the time. But one of these days I must pay for a trip round the Tabernacles, just to say I've done it.'

'Where do you farm?'

'Bartenny.'

'Oh Lord,' said Paul, 'not that wonderful stone house right on top? I've often wondered who was lucky enough to own that. You might as well own an island. There's only the neck where the road turns in, and I notice you've got that well fenced. I'd never make a farmer, but I envy you your habitat, I must say.'

'That neck has been fenced since the Iron Age. I've only put the defences in order. I don't want to be mean, but I don't want to find caravans parked on my corn and town-bred dogs chasing my sheep. And they will, you know, if you give them half a chance. To the usual run of tripper there's no such thing as private property, or if there is, it oughtn't to be allowed. The only defence is to make it physically impossible. Luckily the cliffs do most of the job for me. There's the coastguard path, of course, along the top – that's a public right of way. But I don't mind people walking on the cliff, so long as they don't go in the fields. It's the cars I object to.'

'That's Iron Age, is it, that triple ditch? You can see it clearly from the sea, you know, when the light's right, but I suppose as you never go out you wouldn't have seen. Celtic refugees from just pre-Roman Gaul, wasn't it?'

'The defences? Yes. There were earlier occupations, almost certainly. There's a bunch of round barrows on top of the east cliff which look earlier, though there's no record of their ever having been opened. I haven't done anything about it myself, I'm afraid, but at least I haven't ploughed them down, like most of the farmers round here.'

Dawson looked at his watch and said, 'I must go. Want to get out on the afternoon tide.' He smiled broadly at Bannerman. 'Interesting things, tides,' he said. 'The water goes up and down like anything. You should watch it some time from your cliff castle.'

There was not, Paul decided, any offence in it. It was

71

embarrassing, but no worse. Bannerman smiled it off. 'I will, I promise,' he said. 'Come back safely.' He raised his hand with a friendly casualness as Dawson left them. 'I tell you what,' he said to Paul, 'why don't you and your wife come out and see Bartenny for yourselves? I daren't say so in front of our nautical friend, but I am pathetically proud of it and would love to show you round.'

'We'd love it,' said Paul. 'I rather take it you're not a family man?'

Bannerman smiled again and shook his head. 'Not me,' he said, 'I told you I had put my defences in order. Charles.'

'Yes, Mr Bannerman?'

'How long has Mr Dawson been drinking on this scale? I've seen him down here often enough, but never seen him in this state.'

Charles looked at Paul. 'He's much better than he was, as a matter of fact, Mr Bannerman. Mr Mycroft will confirm that. He's starting to act a bit drunk now at least. A few days ago he'd reached the stage where you couldn't tell.'

'That's a very accurate and cynical observation for a chap of your age. But true, I've no doubt. So long as he's over the worst of it.'

Paul said, 'I don't see any harm in stating the facts. It was Mrs Trent's death upset him. She used to sail with him, and he was a bit sweet on her – enough to make trouble with his wife, anyhow. I walked into the middle of one row myself. Then when she was drowned, apart from missing her, he managed to persuade himself that he was to some extent responsible. Hence the drinking. And hence more rows. It was pretty sad, in fact.'

Bannerman said, 'The one who was washed up on Lanting? I read the inquest report. Damn it, you're the chap that found her. I knew your name rang a bell. But what constructive responsibility did poor old Dawson contrive for himself?'

Paul hesitated. 'I think I'm breaching a drunken confidence,' he said. 'But I do it in confidence, sober, for the man's own reputation. I've no doubt Charles has heard his explanation, anyway. Charles hears everything, but cannot bear the thought of putting it in a book. Mrs Trent used to sail with Dawson regularly. Then Mrs Dawson made trouble and made him promise not to take her sailing again. And the first day, more or less, he didn't she gets drowned. Dawson feels that if only he'd stuck to his guns and had Mrs Trent in his boat as usual, she'd have been all right. What with that and missing her company, he was in a bad way.' He paused and drank. 'Put like that it sounds pretty silly, but the thing was real enough. There was shame, you see, and ignominy, and frustration, and a bit of helpless rage, and a sense of injustice. Agnes had not only taken Millie away from him – she had destroyed her altogether. And he had let her. Not logical, and I suppose morally unsound, but real, bitter and not all that uncommon.'

Bannerman said, 'The classic tragedy of the married man.'

Paul smiled. 'You must ask Charles about that,' he said.

'Charles? What does Charles know about marriage?'

'Not marriage,' said Paul, 'tragedy. Charles sees Dawson as a potentially tragic figure liable to be raised to genuine tragic stature by the death of Mrs Trent. I said he was sad but not tragic, because there was nothing heroic about him. I still think I am right. The tragedy remains potential. I can't see Dawson driven to anything but a bit of mild boozing.'

Bannerman looked from one to the other. 'I wish I had

got into this discussion before,' he said. 'I think I should have enjoyed it. I saw Mrs Trent's death as just one tripper less. I didn't know it had all these implications.'

Charles said, 'Most deaths have, surely. Even the deaths of trippers.'

Bannerman smiled at him. 'I tell you what,' he said to Paul, 'why don't you and your wife come and have dinner with me? I suppose you couldn't join us, Charles? I wish you would. We could go further into the tragedy of Dawson and Mrs Trent.'

'It's very nice of you, Mr Bannerman, but I couldn't get off. My busiest time, you see.'

'I know. Some other time when you're not on duty, perhaps. When could you make it, Mycroft?'

'Any evening, pretty well. Tomorrow, if that's not too soon for you.'

'Tomorrow at seven. Good. Wear whatever you like.'

'Ah,' said Colonel Frayne, 'I thought I recognised the colossal car. The landed gentry. How are you, Bannerman? I haven't seen you before this year.'

A boyish man, thought Paul, as well preserved in his way as his wife and mentally much younger. He had kept himself sweet on a regular, healthy life and a regular, healthy income. He had the bright eye of a schoolboy and a much clearer skin. He must have been good with Susan so long as it was only romps she wanted. For a prop and refuge to the uncertainties of adolescence the mouth was a little unformed. He had already, probably, begun to expect from his daughter the mothering he would himself be expected to provide for his wife. A complicated relationship, whose implications were clearly lost on him. Colonel Frayne had not a care in the world.

He said to Paul, 'I'm jolly glad Sue's making herself useful to Mary. It's good for her, too, to have something to do. She seems to enjoy herself no end with you. She loved your trip yesterday.'

'Did she say so? said Paul. 'I'm glad, anyhow.'

'Not in so many words. They don't at that age. You'll find that later. You have to guess. But I know her pretty well. She likes young company. She's young for her age, you know.'

Bannerman said, 'What was your trip yesterday? Round the Tabernacles? You had the weather for it.'

'That's it. We had young Cardew. He took us through between the Tabernacles and the head – a thing I'd always wanted to do.'

Colonel Frayne said, 'You want the boat for it – and the weather, my goodness. I've never tried. I should think Cardew knows his way about.'

'Mike?' said Bannerman, 'Oh yes, he's all right. His father was famous, of course, in these parts. He was cox-swain of the old lifeboat, before they had their present unsinkable semi-submarine. I imagine the old man taught Mike most of what there is to know about local waters. Anyway, he's never wanted to do anything else. He's a cut above most of them, you know – he could have made good money ashore if he'd wanted to. But if that's how he's happy, good luck to him. I suppose some girl will get her hooks into him presently and try to give him ambitions. I hope he has the guts to tell her where she gets off.'

Paul said, 'Perhaps he's also put his defences in order. I gather from Mary that he'll need them. Or perhaps the boot's on the other foot.'

'Yes. Yes, he's very striking. I should think the women would go for him. But he's a quiet sort of chap. I haven't heard of him as a heart- or home-breaker.' His tone implied mild disapproval.

'I liked him very much,' said Paul.

Colonel Frayne said, 'I haven't seen this local Romeo. Or if I have, I haven't noticed him.'

Paul almost said, 'Ask your wife,' but reconsidered it. Mrs Frayne who was so vague about sergeants, would not in fact have noticed the beauty of a local fisherman. He doubted whether she was particularly attracted to any man. Men were a necessity to her, economically and spiritually, but they would have to be of the right sort. So long as they were that, he thought, almost any man would, for her strictly limited purposes, be acceptable. The others would hardly exist. He said, 'Well, as Bannerman says, he's a quiet sort of chap. And I think he probably works at his job. I can't see him posing on the jetty as part of the holiday attractions. Do you think Susan would help us out tomorrow evening, so that we can take advantage of Bannerman's very kind invitation to dine with him?'

'Oh? Oh yes, I'm sure she will. She's not doing anything. But ask her. She's around somewhere.'

'I will. Anyway,' he said to Bannerman, 'you can assume we'll arrange something. I'm not going to be done out of our visit to Bartenny for lack of a baby-sitter.'

'That's the spirit. See you at seven, then.' He nodded to Colonel Frayne and they went out together. The clients of the Carrack did not run to cheap cars, but even among theirs Bannerman's monster was, as Colonel Frayne had said, conspicuous. Paul heard its deep growl go up the hill as he turned into the hotel to find Susan.

She was sitting in one of the smaller rooms doing, as far as he could see, nothing whatsoever. She did not look at all bored.

'Of course,' she said. 'I'll come out early and give Mary a chance to get herself ready. You're honoured, you know. Daddy will be green with envy. Mr Bannerman's rather a social excitement in these parts.'

76

'Your father knows, as a matter of fact,' said Paul. 'I didn't actually see him turn green. But now I come to think of it, he did seem slightly startled.'

'I bet he was. He wouldn't actually bite his nails, of course. But he'll tell Mummy at lunch. Like to bet?'

'Not with you. You're too observant by half. See you tomorrow evening, then, if not before.'

'That's exciting,' said Mary later. 'I could do with a night out. What do we wear for this educated farmer of yours?'

'He said wear anything you like. Having said that, he won't be wearing a dinner-jacket. He'll probably be wearing something inconspicuous, darkish and ghastly expensive. As he's a bachelor, you won't have his wife's clothes to consider. I should have thought short black for you, as smart as you like but not too full. I'll do the best I can with my second-best office suit. It's all I've got, anyway. I've an idea we shall be very well fed. But the house alone looks worth a visit. Did you know, by the way, that Mike Cardew's father was coxswain of the lifeboat and the local old man of the sea? Young Mike learnt his trade from his father and is said to be wedded to the sea.'

'Seems a waste,' said Mary. 'I expect the mermaids will get him.'

'They'll have to be slightly superior mermaids, I gather – grammar-school at least. That's according to Bannerman, who probably knows. But why should anyone get him? Why can't he go on as he is? He seems to know just what he's doing. So, incidentally, does Bannerman. He is what I call a professional bachelor. He clearly prides himself on it and would rally to the help of any other promising man threatened with matrimony. I'm fairly certain he makes a point of doing himself well in everything and is not averse to people's noticing it. That's why I think we'll be well fed tomorrow. I rather expect everything of the best, with an implied challenge to you, or any woman, to better it if you can. Whether you approve or not, that sort makes the perfect host. I'm looking forward to it.'

'So am I. I am more than willing to be done well, and I am pretty curious about your Mr Bannerman. I must go and brush up the short black.'

CHAPTER NINE

The notice said: THIS IS PRIVATE PROPERTY. NO PARKING, CAMPING OR PICNICKING. WILL THOSE ENTITLED TO ENTER PLEASE SHUT THE GATE AFTER THEM. The gate was steel tubes hung on concrete posts. On either side a short length of dry-stone wall joined the gate to the primeval rampart that stretched away to the cliff's edge. The rampart itself was topped with a concrete and barbed wire fence.

'Lumme,' said Paul, 'that's firm enough, in all conscience. It would need a pretty hard-boiled tripper to ignore that. Unless, of course, he couldn't read, which is always possible nowadays. But the interesting thing is that he has done exactly what he said he had done – put the defences in order. That's where the original gate was, and that bank would have been topped with a palisade. Not barbed wire, of course, even in the Iron Age, but wood and probably some stone. How are we for time?'

'Almost exactly seven.'

'Do you mind if I pop down to the end of the wall? I want to see how he's dealt with the cliff path. You stay in the car, or you'll ruin your shoes.'

He walked down over the sloping sweet-smelling turf. Across the Lanting sands and the wide river mouth the line of headlands fell away south-westwards in a fading

series of greens, purples and misted greys. The wrinkled
sea, still full of sunlight, crawled at his feet. The air was
soft and smelt of paradise. The end of the ancient rampart
had been re-built almost to the edge of the cliff, where a
stile of stone slabs gave access to the coastguard's path.
Here was another notice. It said: PUBLIC RIGHT OF WAY
ALONG CLIFF PATH ONLY. THERE IS NO WAY DOWN TO THE
SEA. THESE CLIFFS ARE DANGEROUS. PLEASE DO NOT ENTER
THE FIELDS, WHICH ARE PRIVATE PROPERTY. This reasonable phrasing was reinforced, Paul noticed, with a six-foot
wire fence between the path and the swelling stubble on
its right. He walked back to the car.

'He's got it all covered,' he said. 'He's not only legal,
he's reasonable. He is also absolutely impregnable. I take
off my hat to him.'

Mary said, 'Dare we open the gate and drive in, do
you think, provided we shut it behind us?''

'I think we might risk it. I expect there'll be guard dogs.'

'That's it. Man-eaters baying alongside the car as we
drive in. A white-faced man will come and whip them in
before we can disembark at the front door. Then when
we pull the iron chain and hear the great bell jangle somewhere in the cavernous depths of the house, the door will
be opened—'

'Not at once it won't. First powerful lights will be turned
on, and we shall be inspected through a heavily barred
grille set high up in the iron-studded door.'

'All right. Then the iron-studded door will be opened
by a sinister and inscrutable man-servant—'

'Ah Wong, a Chinee, whom Bannerman brought back
from his travels in the East and has kept by him ever
since.'

'I hope Ah Wong does the cooking. They always do it so
well.'

'I'm hungry,' said Paul. 'Let's get on.' He swung the iron gate open, noticing without surprise that it was perfectly hung and had grease on its hinges. He drove the car in, stopped and went back to shut the gate.

'Get in quick,' said Mary, 'the dogs will be on us any minute.'

The inner ramparts were not palisaded. The road, tarmac here and of far better quality than outside the gate, ran slightly uphill towards the top of the headland. As the line of the cliffs fell back, the fields broadened out on either side, mostly pasture or new stubble, with dry-stone fences. Then the road dipped slightly and there, in a shallow valley between them and the rocky outline ahead, was the house. It faced west, looking down its dip into the sunset. In this light the granite and slate were honey-coloured. There was no garden, only yards and farm buildings, all of stone, and then the fields.

Paul turned the car into a gravel sweep in front of the house, and a tumult of deep barking burst on them. Clawed feet scrabbled at the sides of the car, and two enormous yellow heads appeared at their elbows. They licked everything they could get at. 'Where's that white-faced man?' said Mary. 'I'm worried about my stockings.' The Labradors fawned on them as they got out.

The door was oak, but there was an electric bell push. There was no grille and no studs. They stood on the step, each scratching a slavering yellow head. 'Never mind,' said Paul, 'I expect we'll hear strange and sinister cries from the inner rooms. Bannerman will frown, Ah Wong will disappear for a minute and the cries will be silenced. Hold everything. Here comes Ah Wong.'

Ah Wong was elderly and wore a soft white apron over a black silk frock. She said, 'Good evening. Will you come in, please? I'll tell Mr Bannerman.' The accent was strongly local. If Bannerman had brought her back from the East, it must have been a long time ago. She got Paul and Mary into the hall without the Labradors, who went on barking and slavering outside. The house smelt faintly of incense, as old churches do, even churches where incense is never used. Everything was perfect, but acquired, as if it had been assembled by an act of deliberate aesthetic judgment, not there from the beginning. But the taste was catholic. There was no period nonsense.

Bannerman was just not wearing a dinner-jacket. His dark coat was double-breasted, but his shirt and collar were faintly striped and his bow tie faintly spotted. He looked extraordinarily impressive. His welcome, like everything else, was perfect. The phrase 'doing the honours' came into Paul's mind. Bannerman was doing the honours. He was even overdoing them. Mary queened it and ruffled her feathers in response, but there was, to Paul's accustomed ear, no mistaking the lack of warmth. She had not taken to Bannerman, not immediately. She was enjoying herself no end, and would let him prove himself if he could. But he was no Cardew.

In a way perhaps, thought Paul, this was no bad thing. The entertainment, as he had guessed, promised to be perfect. He was prepared to give his mind and senses a free hand. It was no great loss if his heart was not touched. He heard the door open behind him and saw Mary, taken off her guard, stare pop-eyed for a moment over his shoulder. Bannerman said, 'Ah, Elizabeth.' He really said, 'Ah.'

Paul swung round as quickly as his glass would permit. 'Mrs Mycroft,' said Bannerman, 'This is Miss Merrion. Liz, Mr and Mrs Mycroft.' Everybody bowed and murmured. Liz was a knock-out. She was one of those golden women, so coloured that she seemed to be modelled entirely out of pliable silver-gilt. Only her eyes were lapis. Mercifully, she wore a short black frock.

Bannerman said, 'Liz comes and does for me on very special occasions. She is a far better cook than you would believe from her appearance.'

'I'm not sure how I should take that,' Miss Merrion said. Her voice was rounded, like the lower registers of the wood-wind. 'I cannot answer for my appearance at the moment. I have just come from the kitchen, and have probably got grease smears on my nose. But I hope Mr and Mrs Mycroft will believe that I am a very serious cook, and very, very expensive.' She gave Paul a devastating smile. 'Anyway, there's only one proof of the pudding. Dinner in about five minutes, Pete. We'll get the signal.'

They took their glasses into the long western window. Either the dip sloped more sharply than Paul had thought, or the window was very cunningly set. There was no foreground to the picture at all. They looked straight on to a shimmering red-gold sea, crossed with an endless procession of curving shadow lines where the Atlantic rollers built up on the shallow foreshore of Lanting Bay. Behind, Skittle Hill stood up black against the sunset.

'Lor,' said Paul, 'magic casements. I can't think how you ever get any work done.'

Bannerman smiled but said nothing. It was a trick he had, effective if you could get away with it. Almost invariably he did get away with it. His smile was very powerful.

They stood in a silent group, their glasses in their hands, flooded with the pink light. They made in their way as fine a picture as the one they looked at.

Something in the house behind them moaned suddenly and heart-rendingly. There was a moment's silence and then whatever it was cried again, a soft cry of complete despair. Bannerman said, 'It's poor Cynthia. She has to be shut up, I'm afraid.'

A deep-voiced bell clanged suddenly, and Paul felt Mary jump at his elbow. The reverberations died away and then, just as the silence became complete, it clanged again. This happened five times. 'Let's eat,' said Bannerman.

Miss Merrion said, 'Shall I lead the way?'

Mary said, 'Oh yes – please do,' as if she had had all the fight knocked out of her. They processed to the door.

The dining-room also faced west, and there were candles burning against the now daffodil sky. Paul found himself in the grip of sheer sensuous excitement, and as the meal progressed, served silently by Ah Wong with some help from Miss Merrion, he surrendered to it completely. It wasn't real, but while it lasted there was no arguing with it. Conversation was low-pitched and limited. Bannerman smiled and smiled. Paul thought, 'He's got us licked, and knows it. That's what he wants, after all. My one duty as a guest is to enjoy myself.' He continued to do so.

It was late in that perfect progression of food and drink that something fumbled and whimpered at one of the panelled doors. Miss Merrion said, 'It's Cynthia. Shall I let her in?'

Bannerman said, 'Better not.' Paul, ready for anything, did not mind either way. The lever kicked suddenly, the door swung open and an enormous black Labrador rolled joyously into the room. Mary said, 'Oh – Cynthia?' on a rising note of near hysteria.

'She's on heat,' said Bannerman. 'May as well let her stay. The dogs are outside.' Cynthia galumphed once round the table and flung herself panting at Bannerman's feet.

Presently Miss Merrion said, 'Shall we go and look for coffee, Mrs Mycroft?' Chairs were pushed back, doors opened and shut, everybody moved suddenly in the light of the low-burning candles. They trod on air, but were perfectly steady on their feet. The table emptied itself of its superfluities, and Bannerman brought out decanters and cigars. He said, 'I hope you enjoyed Liz's cooking as much as I do.'

Paul thought seriously for a moment. The thing was really important to him. 'I'm fairly certain,' he said at last, 'that it was the best meal I've ever eaten. Of course, the wine made a substantial contribution.'

'Good,' said Bannerman. 'The wine is my department, naturally. I'm a bit of a collector.'

'But where in the world did you collect Miss Merrion?'

He knew Bannerman would smile and knew he must accept it if he chose to say nothing. Bannerman smiled. He held up his glass and looked at the candle flame through it. He said, 'Ah.' That's twice, thought Paul. Bannerman said, 'Miss Merrion is a bit of an institution, Mycroft. One has to know that she exists and one has to be – well, in a position to command her services. One can't do it often, of course. As I said, the special occasions.'

'I can only be thankful that you made us your occasion.'

'I wanted to,' said Bannerman. 'To tell the truth, there aren't many people in these parts I am much inclined to exert myself to entertain. I gambled on your being different.'

'I feel different, at the moment, from anyone I have ever known. But that is the result of your invitation and can hardly have been the cause of it.'

'No, but look,' said Bannerman, 'would you invite Frayne or Dawson to a proper meal? Not that Dawson can always be as bad as he is at the moment. I was worried by that. I hadn't heard about it, you know, until you told me.'

'Millie Trent?' Paul tried desperately to rekindle in his mind the tragedy of Millie Trent, but it seemed irretrievably remote from his present experience. 'That's all finished with,' he said.

Bannerman stared into his candle-lit glass.. 'She must have gone in somewhere round here,' he said.

'That's not been established. I didn't think it had been mentioned.'

'I can't help that. I don't really need Dawson to tell me about the tides, you know. I've lived on Bartenny some time, even if I'm not a sailor. If the sea took her that straight to Lanting, she went in off Bartenny somewhere. I've had it happen to a ewe once.'

'All right,' said Paul, 'say she did. We still don't know how or exactly where.'

Bannerman refilled the glasses with a brown rock-steady hand. 'There were people on the cliff that day,' he said. 'I remembered it when I read about it.'

Paul sipped. 'Damn it, Bannerman,' he said suddenly, 'I'm not interested. I know it's wrong, but I'm not. If you want to talk about it, I'll talk about it tomorrow. But not now, do you mind? It's your doing. You've contrived an evening that's been, of its kind, perfect. I don't want it spoilt. I don't care if you saw Agnes Dawson holding Millie's head under water. I don't want to hear about it now. You must see that, or you couldn't—' he waved a hand despairingly in the candle light – 'do all this.'

Bannerman smiled. 'I didn't see Agnes,' he said. 'It was a man. As a matter of fact, I thought at the time it was Dawson, but it can't have been. All right. Let's forget it.'

The drawing-room was almost in darkness. Only the faintest of indirect light glowed downwards from among the ceiling beams. Mary and Miss Merrion sat facing the dark window, the coffee table comfortably between them.

Paul wondered what on earth they had found to talk about. As he crossed the room a single beam of pure white light struck in through the window, lit for a moment the two sleek heads and went out.

'The Carstone light,' said Bannerman from behind him. 'We get it here just round the edge of Skittle. What about coffee for us, Liz?'

He stopped over the table, and again the white light struck inwards, throwing him up in splendid silhouette.

Mary said, 'Paul, we ought really to be going. We can't keep Susan out too late. I wouldn't deprive you of this coffee, but don't linger over it more than you can help.'

'Oh dear,' said Bannerman, 'I wanted to show you the house. But it's not the best time.'

'It's not the occasion,' said Mary. She spoke with a curious decisiveness. 'Speaking for myself, my cup is full.' She screwed her head round and looked up at Bannerman, smiling, as he smiled down at her. 'I don't mean literally, of course. But my capacity for appreciation is over-strained. You must know what I mean.'

He nodded. 'Right. I'm sorry you must go, but you're perfectly right. Perhaps you'll come and see the house some other time.'

Paul drank his coffee, and the faintest sense of future unease crept into him with its black and velvety perfection. Ah Wong had vanished, and Bannerman and Miss Merrion saw them to the door together. To the last everything was graceful. They left them standing there, perfectly elegant against the lit elegance of their background. The car lights picked up the road, and they made off through the salt night air towards the gate in the earthworks. Neither of them said anything.

Paul swung the heavy gate shut behind the stationary car and climbed back into the driving seat. 'I have taken unto me the wings of the morning,' he said.

'So long as you don't drive us into the uttermost parts of the sea.'

'I won't. I've never felt more sober in my life. Just exalted.'

'I know. All the same, watch the road.'

Susan was coiled in the only large chair. They blinked in the ordinary light of their furnished house and she smiled at them. 'Up to expectations?' she said.

'Beyond imagination,' said Paul. 'Have you heard of a Miss Elizabeth Merrion, better known to Mr Bannerman at least, as Liz?'

'No. One of his attendant nymphs?'

'He said she just comes and does for him on occasions. She would just do for me.'

'Not on your life,' said Mary. 'Come on, it's late and we're talking nonsense. How will you get home, Sue? I'd ask Paul to run you back, but he's taken unto him the wings of the morning, and you'll be better off on your feet.'

'I'll walk, of course. It's only a step and it's a fine night. I'll make Daddy's hair curl at breakfast.'

'I've no wish to cause him pain,' said Paul, 'but nothing you can say will exceed the truth. It was perfection.'

'Including Miss Merrion? That's the bit he'll appreciate.'

'Including Miss Merrion, certainly. Pure gold.'

'Gold, anyhow,' said Mary. 'I grant you that. Solid gold.'

Susan put her coat on and tied a scarf over her head. 'While I remember it,' said Mary, 'we're going into Clanbridge tomorrow for the second house at the Palace. It's a Western, with a home-grown thriller first. If you'd like to come, we'll pick you up about fourish.'

'I'm terribly sorry. I can't – I'm going out.' There

was a moment's pause. 'Can you manage?' she said.

'Of course,' said Mary, 'don't give it a thought.'

CHAPTER TEN

'I'd like to see a bit more of Bannerman,' said Paul over breakfast. 'Do you mind?'

Mary sighed. 'Speaking as an Inspector of Taxes?' she said. 'It's up to you, of course. Only you did say you were on holiday. And you said Millie Trent was nothing for you to get involved in.'

'I said I was on holiday with one possible reservation. We picked this place for ourselves, you know that. What is true is that when they knew I was coming here, they asked me to keep half an eye open for something they're interested in. Nothing more than that. It's only that since yesterday I've had an idea that the half-eye might with advantage be turned on our Mr Bannerman. As for Millie, I shouldn't have supposed there was the slightest connection. It's Bannerman who seems determined to bring her in, not me. And I still don't see what the connection can be. I can't say more than that. I can't help being interested. But the main thing isn't my proper pigeon, and you can take my word for it I don't intend to have my holiday spoilt if I can help it.'

'And in the meantime you are disposed to accept Mr Bannerman's invitation to see the house by daylight?'

'Yes, well, he did ask us, didn't he? And I really do want to see the house, apart from other considerations. Don't you?'

'Despite other considerations, so far as I am concerned. But I still do, yes. Let's ask ourselves to tea. I imagine

Miss Merrion will no longer be in attendance, which may spoil the occasion a bit for you.'

'Never mind. Perhaps he'll have a glossy brunette to help Ah Wong toast the buns. But I'm prepared to enjoy myself even without the attendant nymphs. We'll get Susan to take the family out somewhere.'

'If available. She's not available this afternoon, if that's one of the things you remember from last night. She is going out. Slight pause. Can I manage? No further explanation offered. I don't quite know what it means, but it does at least suggest that we can't count on her quite as much as we have been doing. I hope we haven't done anything to upset her. I think she does need us here in a way, apart from the fact that she's very useful to us. I don't want there to be anything wrong.'

'No, but I'm fairly certain that there isn't. Yes, I remember her saying that last night. I was conscious of a slight jolt of suprise, but I'm sure if there'd been any hard feelings, I'd have noticed it. Ephoria makes one sensitive to that sort of thing, though not much inclined to do anything about it. And one has learnt to expect slight jolts of surprise, don't you think? The better she gets to know you, the less simple she allows herself to appear. Do you see what I mean? It's all on her side. It's not a question of your getting to know her; it's a question of her deciding, after due consideration of your credentials, to let you approach a step or two nearer. She's a deep one, our Susan. I like her very much. But she's not the simple sensitive teen-ager I thought I was rescuing originally.'

An hour later, with a reflective breakfast inside him and his pipe drawing pleasantly, Paul sauntered down between the tamarisks towards the Lanting car-park. His hands were in his pockets and his eyes on the ground. Every now and then, when one particularly asked for it, he kicked a pebble in front of him till he lost it between the tamarisk roots.

He came to the telephone box at the corner of the car-park and passed it with elaborate unconcern. It was empty. He walked to the end of the dune and looked out across the almost level sweep of the bay. Hardly anyone was down yet. The sea was a bright early-morning blue, but already the sun caught the nape of his neck with a promise of heat to come.

He stooped and picked up a pebble. It was smooth, white and perfectly symmetrical. He spun it in the air, called heads, caught it and surveyed it gravely as it lay in his palm. Its faces were still quite indistinguishable. He nodded, dropped it in his pocket and walked quickly back across the car-park.

The box smelt of stale seaweed. He called a London number, asked for the man he wanted and spoke quickly for a minute or less. He spoke in parables, but with no fear of being misunderstood. Then he made his way back to the house.

It was not until the quiet hour of the afternoon that he put his head round the door of Charles's bar. He was clearly too late. Everything was orderly, polished and perfect, and the rolling shutter that guarded the bottles was down.

He backed out almost into the arms of the manageress. She looked at him with a slightly calculating eye. She said, 'I'm afraid the bar's closed, Mr Mycroft. It is Mr Mycroft, isn't it?'

'Yes,' said Paul. 'Yes, I realise the bar's closed. I was really looking for Charles.'

'Well – he's off duty now, of course. And I expect he's out. He generally is in the afternoon.'

'I suppose you've no idea where I could find him?'

She bridled defensively. Charles was evidently one of her protégés. She said, 'Well. He takes his books out as a rule when it's fine like this. He's such a hard-working boy.'

'I know,' said Paul. 'But I don't think I'll worry him. As a matter of fact, I want to go on with a discussion we were having in here the other day. It's difficult to talk to him when he's on the job.'

She softened a bit. 'He generally goes in the dunes, as a matter of fact. He says it's the only place there's any quiet. You could see if you could find him. But don't tell him I said so, or he won't thank me.'

'I won't,' said Paul. 'I'll come on him by chance, if at all. And I promise I won't upset him. Thank you for telling me.'

'That's all right, Mr Mycroft. If you're a friend of his.' She bustled off.

The dunes had few attractions for the seaside visitor. They were difficult walking and had, for all their unearthly quality, nothing of the sea about them. Every now and then the miniature valleys opened to give glimpses of the river mouth and the wooded slopes up-stream of Skittle. The sea was near enough, and the air smelt of nothing else. But the dunes were no man's land. Whatever the sea had done to them, it now left them alone; and the people, who came because of the sea, followed suit.

Paul climbed laboriously up the shifting slope of sand, reached the top and started down the other side. The rounded ridge, with its stubble of hard green spikes, rose behind him, shutting him off from the populous world of Pelant. The peace which Charles came there to find enfolded him suddenly with an unlooked-for sweetness. For the second time that day, he cursed the professional conscience that drove him. But he walked on. If chance brought him to Charles, he would do what he had to do.

91

If not, he was still enjoying himself.

Blurred tracks ran here and there over the humped, impassive landscape. He looked at them with an appraising eye, but could not tell who had made them or when. He made for what looked like a central plateau and from there surveyed the surrounding desolation. He saw no one. More than half relieved, he turned and made for the river. At the summit of the last ridge he forced his way between two fringes of green and almost stepped on the edge of a spread towel. The figure on the towel sat up.

Paul said, 'I'm awfully sorry – oh, hullo, Charles.'

Charles was wearing only a pair of white shorts, and Paul noticed, for some reason with slight surprise, that he was sunburnt and well set up. He said, 'Oh, it's you. I'm sorry I got in your way.' Out in the sandhills, Paul noticed, he did not call him Mr Mycroft.

'It's not for you to apologise,' he said. 'I'm the intruder.'

'I don't think so, really. We have intruded on each other. And that, of course, makes the intrusion absolute. If you were a wandering picnic party or a hand-in-hand couple, I could grunt and ignore you. As it is, if you walk away carefully in another direction, we shall both be so monstrously conscious of respecting each other's solitude that there will be no peace for either of us. We've had our solitude for the day.'

Paul sat down and took out his pipe. 'I agree,' he said. 'That being so, may I stay and talk? You're not working?' The books were there on the towel, but unopened.

'No. Do.'

'Tell me about Bannerman,' said Paul.

'Bannerman? You should be able to tell me. Was the dinner a success?'

'It was fabulous. Did you know he did things on that scale?'

'Numbers, do you mean?'

'Oh no. Only Mary and myself and an extraordinarily beautiful young woman who seemed to be hired for the occasion.'

'A sort of *hetaira?*'

'Or geisha, perhaps. She also did the cooking and acted as hostess. Both perfectly.'

'I wish I'd been there. Has he any conversation, or does he just smile?'

'There wasn't much conversation really. It wasn't so much a social occasion as a sort of entertainment. But the entertainment was so good, it didn't matter. He smiled all right. He puzzles me. Have you seen much of him?'

'Not much. He comes in occasionally, and the visitors cluster round him. You heard Colonel Frayne's approach. But mostly he smiles and keeps his distance.'

'Have you ever known him invite anyone else?'

'Very occasionally. But he's pretty choosey, and the others are furious.'

'We are honoured,' said Paul. 'You too, of course. He wanted you to come.'

'Oh yes. He hadn't noticed me before. I told you I don't get involved.'

'Could he have known Mrs Trent, do you think?'

Charles looked at him sharply. He said, 'He made it perfectly clear he didn't. You heard him.'

'I know. But he seems pretty interested in her death.'

'I thought he was more interested in what we were making of it.'

'I don't think so. Could he have known her?'

'I never saw them meet. I can't guarantee they didn't. It doesn't seem to be my business. I don't want to be rude, but is it yours?'

Paul said, 'I'm not sure yet. It might be. But you'll have

tu take my word for that, I'm afraid.'

Charles thought for a moment. 'I don't think I can tell you anything of significance about Bannerman. What else do you want?'

'Could you give me the order of events on that Wednesday?'

Charles looked at him again. 'You're quite serious in this?' he said.

'Yes,' said Paul.

'All right.' He rolled over on his front and stared at the sand. 'I last saw Mrs Trent just before lunch,' he said. 'She was in my bar. So were a lot of other people, of course. It is one of the busiest times. I can't tell you exactly who else was there. Probably Dawson for one. Not Major Trent, because when he asked about her later in the day, he said he hadn't seen her since breakfast, and I remember checking back in my mind and agreeing that although she had been in the bar before lunch, he had not. I can't tell you when she left or who with. There is no general, concerted move to lunch. The Carrack doesn't believe in hustling its guests. A gong rings, and after that people say at intervals, "Well, what about a spot of food?" ' – Charles's voice, Paul noted, was nicely compounded of the clipped, or Frayne, speech and the more expansive style of Jolly Jack Dawson – 'and then they drift out singly or in groups. I stayed in the bar tidying up after they had all gone.'

'You didn't see her go out of the hotel?'

He shook his head. 'I couldn't have. There is that small room, you know, between the bar and the hall. Where Mrs Dawson used to stage her rows with her husband, if she could manage it.'

'I know. I walked into one.'

'Someone generally did. That's why she did it.'

'As bad as that?'

Charles nodded but said nothing. Then he said, 'I'm off duty during the afternoon, as you know. I was out here, as a matter of fact. But I can tell you this much. There was no racing that afternoon. The tide had been high late in the morning and was falling fast by the time they had finished lunch. But of course you can get a boat off the beach, especially the club boats, any time until nearly full low and do your sailing out in the river mouth. I know, because Fred told me, that Major Trent took one of the club boats single-handed and went out sailing during the afternoon. He came back on the evening flood.'

'That was before he asked about his wife?'

'Oh yes, certainly. There was no question, I mean, of his asking about her and then taking a boat out to look for her. Whether he was looking for her before he asked, of course, I can't say.'

'Let's follow Major Trent through for the moment. When did he ask about her?'

'So far as I am concerned, in the evening before dinner. He came into the bar. It was fairly early. I think there were other people in the bar, but it was before the rush.'

'Did he – how shall I put it? – ask you confidentially, or so that the other people could hear?'

'Oh, quite openly. Yes, I remember, now you ask that. There were other people there, but no one of their particular gang. Otherwise they'd have said something, and I'm sure no one did. But there were people there. He came in deliberately but – I don't know, I got an impression of suppressed urgency. As if he had almost run into the hotel and then checked himself before he came into the bar. I can't swear he was actually out of breath, but that was rather the impression he gave me. He came in—'

'One moment. You say he looked as if he had run into

the hotel. Do you know that he had just come in?'

'No, I can't swear to it. I know for a fact he can't have been in long, because of the time he brought the boat back. But I can't swear that he hadn't, for instance, gone up to their room first. On the other hand, anyone who knows the hotel might well, if he came back to it looking for some-one at that time of the evening, turn straight into my bar to ask. It's a sort of assembly point.'

'Yes. I see. Anyhow, he came in.'

'He came in, as I say, quite deliberately. I think he looked round the bar to see who was there. But then nearly everyone does that, unless it's pretty crowded. Then they just make their way to the bar or join one of the groups. Anyway, he came to the bar. I probably said good evening and asked him what he was going to drink. My usual pro-fessional greeting, you know. He didn't reply. Instead he said, "Have you seen Mrs Trent anywhere? I haven't seen her all day, and there's something I've got to ask her about." Something like that, anyway. I said I hadn't. He nodded. He didn't say anything more. He looked round the bar again, hesitated a moment and then went out.'

'This impression of urgency. Can you be more specific?'

'Not really. The impression I got was that he did want to get hold of his wife urgently, but didn't want to let the urgency appear. But then that's natural enough. No one who has temporarily mislaid his wife is going to rush into a public room panting and say, "My God, have you seen my wife?" Anyone would try to make the enquiry sound casual.'

'Did it strike you as odd that he should ask for her at all?'

'Well – I hadn't heard him do it before. They lived on this curious semi-detached basis. Neither of them ever seemed particularly interested in the other's movements.

No, I just thought that something urgent had arisen and he found himself in the unusual position of wanting to get hold of her quickly. As I say, I got this impression of urgency, excitement of some sort, veiled, but not quite successfully, under an appearance of casualness. But I really couldn't say what sort of excitement it was or what it was about.'

'Did you see him again that evening?'

'No, not at all.'

'What about the other enquiries he is supposed to have made?'

'I didn't hear them myself. But I think someone said something in the bar about it later in the evening. At any rate, I know I got the impression that he'd been making enquiries and that people knew he had.'

'But nobody knew where she was?'

'Apparently. There was a certain amount of archness. You know – no one saying outright "I wonder who she's gone off with this time?" but a sort of general "You know what Millie is" atmosphere.'

'Yes. Now what about Dawson?'

'Dawson was almost certainly in the bar before lunch, but not, I am pretty certain, in the Mrs Trent group. Mrs Dawson was with him. Yes, I remember now. I noticed them because it wasn't usual for her to join him in the bar. In fact, I think that's the only time I've ever seen her there. He came up rather sheepishly and got a gin or something for himself and something soft for her. Normally he'd have been in the thick of the party round Mrs Trent.'

'And I imagine they went out together?'

'I didn't notice, but you can pretty well take it that she hauled him off to have lunch soon after the gong went.'

'What were his movements later?'

'I don't know, but I'm fairly certain he sailed during

the late afternoon or evening. I saw him in the bar before dinner.'

'Before or after Trent's visit?'

'After, definitely. As I said, Trent came in quite early. Dawson came in about the usual time, when the bar was filling up. He looked dreadful.'

'Had he been drinking?'

'Not when he came in, but he soon put that right.'

'No Agnes this time?'

'No. By this time Mrs Trent was known to be out some-where, and I remember thinking that Mrs Dawson evidently saw no need to chaperone him. She was probably lying in wait for him outside.'

'In what way did he look dreadful?'

'Hard driven, as if the devil was after him. He even looked over his shoulder at times, as if he expected God knows what to come in through the door. And as I say, he drank. Not socially, but a real systematic soaking, as if he couldn't bear to stay sober.'

'Did anyone notice this, do you suppose?'

'I can't say. The bar was full, and I was busy. Looking after Dawson alone was one man's job.'

'What did you think yourself?'

'I assumed it was his wife, of course. If she'd been found later in their room with a pillow over her face, I shouldn't have been all that surprised. I rather wish it had been that.'

'He didn't say anything to suggest what the trouble was?'

'I don't think so. The point is, you see, he was more or less alone, drinking alone. Mind you, he may have passed the time of day with one or two other people as a matter of form, but in the main he simply stood at the bar and asked for another every time he caught my eye.'

'Have you ever known him drink this way before?'

'Not like that, no. He always drinks a good deal in relation to his capacity, if you know what I mean. I have seen him more or less ginned-up more often than most of his lot. But his usual line is to be the life and soul of the party. He's always calling for rounds and so on, and he hasn't got a very strong head. But this was quite different. I mean, I felt at once that there was something wrong.'

'But you can't say what?'

'No. Only this air of – I don't know, apprehension, expectancy. Perhaps as if he was waiting for something and couldn't bear to face it sober. But I may be imagining that.'

'That's what you meant when you said that if Agnes had been found murdered you wouldn't have been particularly surprised?'

'Yes. But you do understand, don't you, that this wasn't the only possible sort of explanation? He might equally well have been the traditional devoted husband whose wife was having a baby upstairs.'

'Yes. So what it comes to is that he had lunch here with Agnes, took a boat out single-handed during the late afternoon and was in here probably pretty soon after he got back. Could anyone say when he went out?'

'Only by chance. He's got his own boat. Someone may have noticed.'

'Could he have walked out to Bartenny head and back between lunch and taking his boat out?'

'I shouldn't think so, not without making himself very late for the tide. I don't know where his boat is, but if he'd left it too late, he couldn't have got her out single-handed.'

'Whereas Major Trent is known to have taken a club boat out some time during the afternoon?'

'Yes. It could be pretty late with a club boat, as I said.'

'That's right. And you reckon you saw him fairly soon after he got back. But he wasn't here at lunch time. So far as you're concerned, he could have been anywhere up to the time he went sailing?'

'So far as I'm concerned, yes. But there may be any number of people who know where he was. It's only a matter of asking – if you want to ask.'

'Yes.' He looked at his watch. 'For the moment I must concern myself with the *Lone Rider of Q Range*.'

'At the Palace?' Charles was all interest at once. 'I've seen it. It's rotten.'

'You have?' said Paul. 'Good Lord, you do surprise me.'

Charles brushed the sand carefully off the edge of his towel and turned over on his back. He said to the sky, 'I am interested in tragedy in all its forms.'

Paul said, 'Ah.' He picked his way back over the sand dunes towards Pelant.

CHAPTER ELEVEN

'How did he take it?' said Mary.

'Momentarily distinctly shaken, I thought. Then he pulled himself together in the face of a fresh challenge to his bachelordom. The perfect bachelor, obviously, must be every child's perfect uncle. He said of course, he'd be delighted. Hoped they wouldn't be too bored. We must find something to amuse them. I didn't say that what they would be mainly interested in was the food, because of course that's the first thing he'd think of. He'll no doubt turn Ah Wong on to doing a cream tea.'

'If he gives them a cream tea on the scale he gave us dinner, they certainly won't be bored, whatever else they are. And Ah Wong will love it. She probably longs for the patter of tiny feet at Bartenny.'

'I think that's extremely doubtful. Anyhow, it's on. You

can tell them we are all invited to tea. I shall be interested to see what they make of him.'

'Cathleen's reaction will be the interesting one. Jennifer will take advantage of his obvious desire to please and will ride him for all she's worth. Cathie will take more persuading. Anyway, a farm's always a farm. And there are the dogs.'

'Lord, yes, it's not them I'm worrying about, it's him.'

'I should say that so long as they're obviously enjoying themselves, he'll be happy. That's what he wants, after all.'

'I agree. Four o'clock tomorrow, then. Clean, but not party. He'll be in working clothes, he says.'

'That should be worth seeing. He probably has his overalls cut in London.'

This time there were no dogs. What struck them most, in daylight, was the house's perfection in detail. As a house of that age and type could hardly fail to be, it was beautiful in its own right, and would be beautiful in the last stages of decay. But it was perfectly maintained. The old stone was recently but unobtrusively pointed, the slates faultlessly aligned. Wherever paint was needed, it was new, thick and glossy. It was professional work, done to order.

Ah Wong too was professional, welcoming but not expansive. She ran a quick appraising eye over the children, who stared back at her solemnly from under the stone arch of the doorway. She said, 'Good afternoon. Mr Bannerman said to tell you he'll be in very shortly. He said would the children like to see the calves till he's ready?'

Mary said, 'Oh yes, they'd love it.' They trooped out in silence through a stone-flagged passage, and the afternoon hung in the balance. A shaft of dusty sunlight lit the calf-house from one side and bodies stirred in the shadowed straw. Then Cathleen said, 'Oh look,' and ran forward. Through the wooden barrier the enchanted fawn-faces of infant Jerseys stared at them, their black noses polished and expectant. They had the daft beauty of debutantes. Jennifer said nothing but climbed the barrier and knelt in the straw with her arms round the nearest neck.

'She'll smell,' said Paul.

'Never mind,' said Mary, 'so long as they enjoy it. It was touch and go.'

Paul said, 'Keep them here for a minute, will you? I just want to have a look round.'

The house was a simple rectangle with a small back wing probably housing modernisations. The farm buildings, closely grouped, proclaimed their uses and stood open for inspection. There was no one about. Paul went from one to the other, judging the interiors with a practised eye. A garage-workshop held the black monster he had last seen outside the Carrack, and in one corner a flight of stone steps led upwards to a trap-door. He dodged outside again. The building was high, with a steeply pitched roof. He looked round and still saw no one. The trap-door seemed to be locked, though he could not see a fastening. He pushed at it again.

Bannerman said, 'There's a tower-bolt in the corner – if you look.' He stood at the bottom of the steps looking up. He was smiling and quite motionless.

'Lord,' said Paul, 'I'm so sorry. I find these buildings wonderfully interesting, and you have them in beautiful condition. I wanted to see the roof timbers. It's a very steep pitch.'

Bannerman said, 'Go on in and look.' He still did not move.

'Not now you've come,' said Paul. 'Mary and the children will be wondering where we are.'

'It's quite empty,' said Bannerman. 'We don't use that loft except in emergencies. The view of the roof timbers is uninterrupted.'

Paul came down the steps. 'They're with the calves,' he said.

They walked to the calf-shed in silence, the Labradors cavorting round them. Bannerman apologised to Mary for being late, smiled wordlessly at the children and began to talk about the calves. He was going to be good. He talked to the children as though they were ignorant but interested adults. He told them ages and pedigrees, how the animals were related, what their particular faults and virtues were and where they stemmed from. Only the Labradors were introduced by name. Finally he said, 'What about tea?'

Jennifer, her arms on the wooden barrier and her head on her arms, said, 'Why are they all girl-calves?'

'Heifers,' he said. 'Because they will give milk and I make money selling it.'

'What happens to the boys?'

'Bulls. Most of them are killed for meat.' No apology was offered or, apparently, required.

'I'd like tea now,' said Jennifer.

He nodded. 'Tea's in the old kitchen.' They trooped inside. The floor was flagged and the table bare and bleached deal. Not here, clearly, had Miss Merrion done her exquisite work, but in some modernised inner sanctuary. For tea it was perfect. They pulled out the benches and there was a moment of awe-struck silence. Mary had been right. Ah Wong, or somebody, had done her best. Cathleen said, 'But Mummy—'

Jennifer said, 'Is all that cream?'

Bannerman nodded smiling. 'You said you ate cream teas,' he said to Paul.

'Did I? Heaven forgive me, I believe I did. I didn't know what I was talking about. I am now about to for the first time in my life.'

Bannerman said to Mary, 'You too, I hope?'

'All of us, according to our capacities and probably beyond them. You aren't going to nibble a biscuit and drink black tea, are you?'

He smiled and shook his head. 'I like cream,' he said. They set to.

Presently he said, 'Can they be left to finish the course by themselves?'

The crockery was old and beautiful but not fabulous. 'Oh yes,' said Mary. 'All right, Cathie?' Cathleen nodded.

'Then would you like to have a look at the house now, and we can all walk round the head afterwards?'

'That sounds admirable,' said Paul.

The rooms were fewer and larger than they had expected, and only two of the bedrooms had more than token furnishings. There was nothing of the museum about it. Everything was for use, and they saw nothing that would not be a pleasure to use. The golden air blew gently in between the stone mullions, and in all the upstairs rooms the farm smells, faint but reassuring, were mixed with the smell of the house itself and the perennial exhalation of cliff and sea.

'How long have you been here?' said Paul.

'It must be fifteen years, I suppose. I came here soon after the war.'

'It must be wild in the winter,' said Mary.

He smiled. 'Only outside.'

'Do you know,' said Paul, 'I think if I lived here, I should never go on the sea. If it's any comfort to you, I don't share Dawson's view on that. The sea – down there, all round you – is part of the natural walls of your world.

104

It is unavoidable, but does not call for closer investigation. I fancy people who live among mountains seldom climb them. It's the visitors who climb.'

Mary said, 'I'd want to swim in it.'

Bannerman nodded. 'I do swim,' he said, 'but not – not in this sea, if you see what I mean. Not in my sea. For one thing, you can't – you can't get at it. I drive down off Bartenny to some place where the sea comes to meet you, and then I swim in it. I suppose for that matter I could sail on it if I wanted to. But it's not the same sea.'

'You're an islander, of course,' said Paul. 'It's a different mentality.'

Bannerman shrugged. 'It suits me,' he said.

He showed them everything, every cupboard and corner and bend of the stairs. Paul, busy with a mental measuring rod, knew that all the space between the walls was being accounted for. The upstairs rooms were built well up into the pitch of the roof, with sloping ceilings at front or rear and a flat hung under the ties of the rafters. Bannerman said, 'There's not much roof-space, as you can see.' He stopped in the central passage and pulled down counter-weighted steps. 'Like to see the roof timbers?' he asked Paul. 'There's lighting in the roof.' Paul, suddenly possessing himself of the enemy's weapons, smiled broadly and shook his head, but said nothing. On the ground floor they found, as he had anticipated, a small and exquisite working kitchen and beyond it a blank door heavily padlocked. Bannerman unlocked it and put down a switch. Row upon row, bin behind bin, the bottles gleamed dully in the dim light. 'My collection,' he said. 'It's a stone room specially lined. But there is thermostatic control for emergencies.'

'No cellars?' said Paul.

He shook his head and smiled. 'Never in these parts. The house is put straight on to the rock. A cellar would

105

have had to be cut by quarrymen. And then it would probably strike water.' He looked at Paul and smiled again. 'Anyone will tell you the same,' he said.

The silence was absolute as they came back along the flagged passage towards the kitchen. 'I hope they're all right,' said Mary.

'Stupefied,' said Paul. 'They don't want to speak and probably can't.' The three faces turned slowly to meet them as they opened the door. They wore the rapt expression of those who have been united in some great spiritual experience. Bannerman ran a calculating eye over the table. 'I must say,' he said, 'it's pretty impressive. Will they be all right?'

'So long as they can walk they'll survive.'

'Lavatory and wash-basin in there,' said Bannerman, pointing. The three children disentangled themselves from the benches and went tentatively out.

'You think of everything,' said Mary.

Bannerman smiled. 'All flesh is as grass,' he said.

They came out of the yards into the open fields and turned left along a path that skirted the far side of the dip. Beyond the last field the wire fence stood up threateningly against the sky. Bannerman unlocked a gate, and they came out on to the cliff path. Below them the cliff fell away sharply in patches of gorse and brambles and then stopped short against a background of distant, crawling sea. It was completely quiet.

'It's a long way round,' said Bannerman. 'Are they good for it?'

'It will be good for them,' said Paul.

Mary said, 'Are there any dangerous places?'

'Not if you stay on the path. It never gets within slipping distance of the edge. To go much below the path isn't safe. Let them go ahead and you come after them.

Otherwise you'll worry. Your husband and I will bring up the rear.'

'All right. Cathie, you go ahead and take Julia. There's room for the two of you. Then you, Jennifer. And nobody leave the path.'

'Off we go, then,' said Paul. They went.

At times they had thirty yards of tangled slopes on their left hand. At others a hummock of jagged rock shut them in, or the path dropped suddenly into a seaward dip as steeply pitched as the valley-gutter of an enormous roof. Whatever the land did, it never visibly reached the sea. Always at some point it broke off short without explanation, and they sensed, but never saw, the treacherous overhanging lip and below it the black vertical drop to the invisible and silent sea.

'Is there no way down?' said Paul.

'Not without ropes and all the proper gear. Neither up nor down. Wrecks on Bartenny were always regarded locally as an economic disaster. It is true the loss of life was satisfactorily complete, but the spoils were irrecoverable until the sea moderated enough to get boats out. And by then, of course, most of it was lost. There is a small cove round the head on the Bartenny Bay side where you can beach a boat in the proper weather, and the beach is yours between half-ebb and half-flood. But you can't get off it, and it never gets any sun except in the early mornings, so it's not an ideal picnic spot.'

Paul said, 'Your Iron Age visitors knew what they were about. It's the perfect natural fortress.'

'That's it. They picked it from the sea, of course. They must have come in in still weather and rowed round it. You can imagine them all pointing up at the grimmer features and jabbering excitedly in Q-Celtic. I suppose they landed in force on Lanting or somewhere and marched up to take possession. Once they'd got the neck fortified, Bartenny was theirs against all reasonable comers. There's no saying what numbers it supported. In any case, I expect they went out and took what they wanted from the locals, just as I get my groceries from Pelant or Clanbridge.'

'I bet before a couple of summers were out the locals were charging them an extra fourpence a dozen for eggs. And I suppose the legions caught up with them in the end.'

'I imagine so. An army which had got into Maiden Castle wouldn't need to detach much strength to deal with my triple ditch. But they must have had a few years of splendid isolation, despite the price of eggs. My tenure rests on different foundations, of course, but even I feel reasonably secure. I don't think they'd put a housing estate on Bartenny. It wasn't even big enough or flat enough for a fighter station.'

The path rose sharply in front of them and all at once the fields gave up the struggle and the wire fence fell away to their right and was left behind. Lichened and weatherworn, the essential granite broke out of its thin covering of turf and thrust its head out into the Atlantic. The children were short-winded from their tremendous tea, and the pace slackened as they climbed steadily towards the top. They were there quite suddenly. The path ducked right-handed under the scarred rock and there was nothing ahead of them but sea and sky and below, pyramid-based on the remote sea surface, the black and green pile of the Tabernacles.

'Golly,' said Cathleen, and the party came to a halt.

A gull floated nonchalantly by them, turning a quick sideways eye for the possibility of food. Seeing nothing to detain him, he stood suddenly on his right wing-tip and fell away in a long curve to the green top of the Tabernacles, where he sat and ruffled his neck feathers. An invisible ship threw up a cloud of smoke on the almost white horizon, and between, tiny and remote, a fishing boat toiled imperceptibly against the vast eastward movement of the sea.

Bannerman unzipped his jacket and brought up a pair of small but exquisite binoculars on a lanyard. 'I think—' he said. 'Yes, now I've got him. I may be wrong, but I think that's your friend Cardew.'

'Mr Cardew! ' said Cathleen in an ecstasy.

Jennifer said, 'May I see?'

Bannerman smiled at her but shook his head. 'I'm afraid not, Jennifer. As a matter of fact, I don't think you'd see much. These glasses aren't easy to use and they're very easy to break. So I make it a rule never to lend them. Sorry.'

For a moment Jennifer looked steadily into his smile. Then she nodded and turned seawards again. Bannerman said, 'He's got someone with him, I think, which is unusual for him.'

Cathleen said, 'Is it a girl?'

Bannerman shook his head. 'I couldn't tell at this distance,' he said. 'I shouldn't think so. I hope not anyhow.' He smiled at Paul.

'Someone getting her hooks in him and giving him ambitions?' said Paul.

'Lor, yes,' said Mary, 'the grammar-school mermaid.'

'It had legs,' said Bannerman. 'I didn't see any hooks. It was human. But whether male or female I can't say. It wasn't wearing a crinoline, of course, or anything distinctively feminine. We could always ring up the coastguard station and ask them for a ruling. They have a very powerful glass and ought to know a mermaid when they see one.'

'I think we might leave it speculative,' said Paul. 'That

109

will give everyone pleasure of a sort.' They resumed their walk.

'Careful, Cathie,' said Mary. For fifteen, perhaps twenty, yards the curving path seemed to hang right over the sea. The green slope below it was rough and full of handholds, but it went down almost vertical to the edge of the drop. Then the path turned right-handed again round the shoulder of the headland and began to fall steadily. The stretch of green on their left lengthened and flattened out, and the piled rocks fell away until they ducked under the turf. The wire fence joined them from the right and they were walking once more alongside the stubble. The headland proper was behind them and the green and gold stretches of Bartenny broadened in front.

It was an odd leave-taking. The wings of the morning, Paul thought, were noticeably lacking at this time of the late afternoon. The place was pure magic, despite the new paintwork and the careful pointing of the stones. But their minds could not surrender to it.

Bannerman smiled and said, 'You must come again next year,' but Paul knew, and knew that Bannerman knew, that they would not come to Bartenny again. Mary said, 'We've all loved it,' and Bannerman shook hands with the children, smiling and saying nothing. They got themselves into the car, and as it started Bannerman waved his hand and went off, his Labradors clustering round him. For a moment Paul saw him in the driving mirror, and was conscious of a cold rush of discomfort, like the mental adjustment that brings down the curtain on a play.

Mary said, 'Are you feeling all right after your tea?' and the children said yes, it had been lovely and reminded each other of the excitements of the afternoon until Cathleen said suddenly, 'Poor Mr Bannerman.'

'Why poor?' said Paul. 'I should have thought he'd got

everything anyone could want.'

'I know. I don't think he wanted us there.'

Mary said, 'He did you well anyhow.'

'I like him,' said Jennifer. 'It didn't matter about the glasses.'

Cathleen said, 'Oh I know. It wasn't his fault. It would have been better if you and Daddy had gone alone, really.'

'I'm sorry,' said Paul. 'That was my idea. I was glad to have you, in fact.'

'Oh well,' said Cathleen, 'it was worth trying. And it was a lovely tea, as you say.'

The car turned out on to the coast road, and they made for Lanting.

CHAPTER TWELVE

The sergeant said, 'Good morning, Mr Mycroft' suddenly at his elbow.

Paul, who had been wondering whether he ought to buy doughnuts or sugar buns, was startled by an overwhelming sense of guilt. He said, 'Oh hullo, sergeant. Shall I buy doughnuts or those white buns, do you think?'

'Better the doughnuts, sir, I'd say. They travel better and they'll all look alike by tea-time. With the buns losing sugar the way they do, you'll have a job to even them out, if you understand me. And then there's always likely to be trouble.'

'A Solomon,' said Paul. 'I hate to think of the years of suffering that must lie behind that lightning apprehension. You're right, of course. Doughnuts it is.'

'If you've not much more to get, I'm just going out your way. Or have you got the car?'

'I haven't. The family have. I'd like a lift very much, if you can manage it.'

The sergeant nodded. 'I'll pick you up here,' he said.

'You've been visiting Mr Bannerman, I see,' said the sergeant, as the car joined the queue at the level crossing.

Paul looked at him with apprehension. 'Are we, too, under observation?' he said.

The sergeant smiled. 'If we was to keep all our visitors under observation,' he said, 'we'd need half the county force down here.' He thought. 'Not but what,' he said, 'we might pick up some interesting things, but not much in the way of serious crime, perhaps. No, the truth is, I happen to see your car come out of the Bartenny turning the other evening, and I didn't see what else you'd be doing there at that time of the night but visiting Mr Bannerman. He doesn't have many visitors, in fact, so I was apt to notice.'

'I hope,' said Paul, 'that you observed the great skill and circumspection of my driving. I had, as a matter of fact, taken unto me the wings of the morning.'

'Well,' said the sergeant. 'Well, it wasn't too bad considering. I came along behind you, in fact, for a bit. Just in case of accidents, if you see.'

'Damn it, we have been under observation. Take what proceedings you will, but don't tell my wife. She didn't think much of my wings either.'

'Ah, I see you had Mrs Mycroft with you, of course, so I reckoned you'd be all right. I'm told Mr Bannerman keeps a good table, but as I say, he don't entertain much as a rule.'

'As any man in Italy,' said Paul. 'As a matter of fact, we were up there again yesterday afternoon with the family.'

'Were you now? You're honoured, by the sound of it.'

'So I have been told. He's an odd man, wouldn't you say?'

112

A cloud of steam moved slowly across the tops of the cars ahead. The engine, though audible, was too small to be seen, but the tops of a pair of coaches and some miscellaneous rolling-stock went by, and the queue stirred with expectancy.

'Odd, you'd say, would you?' said the sergeant. 'Well, I don't know. Very respectable man, Mr Bannerman, though he keeps himself to himself.'

'What's he like as a farmer? Of course, he's a bachelor and all that, but he seems to have plenty of money to spend.'

The sergeant smiled as the car crawled off on the tail of the car in front. 'He's learnt a bit, I'm told, since he come here. Didn't know much then, by all accounts. But he works at it all right, and of course the money helps. He's got all the machinery in the world.'

'Private means, I imagine? He doesn't make all that from the farm, surely?'

'Would seem so. Quite a wealthy man, I'd say. Not but what the farm must pay quite well with all he puts into it.'

Paul said, 'Did he know Mrs Trent, do you know?'

The sergeant looked at him for a moment and then again at the traffic ahead. 'Not that we ever heard,' he said. 'Did you think he did, then, sir?'

'I've no evidence that he did. He did say he thought she must have gone into the water somewhere round Bartenny, the set of the currents being what it is. I was interested, because I don't remember that coming out at the time. But of course, he's in a position to know. He also said he thought he remembered seeing people on the cliffs that day.'

'When did he say this, then, sir?'

'Well – he happened to be in the Carrack bar when I was talking to some people about her death. He seemed

113

interested, but of course it wasn't him that started the subject. And then later when we dined with him he volunteered the observation about her having gone in round Bartenny. There wasn't much more to it than that. I'll tell you what started it. It was Mr Dawson. He was drinking hard. He'd been badly upset by Mrs Trent's death and had been in trouble with his wife about it. You know he was sweet on her. Bannerman asked what was wrong with him and that brought the subject up. He said he'd seen the inquest report but hadn't taken much notice of it.'

'Well then – he couldn't have known her, could he, sir?' He turned and gave Paul a rather fierce stare.

Paul, bland in his turn, smiled back at him. 'Not on his account of it, no,' he said.

'Well, sir, we've never heard anything to connect him with the lady. He's a bachelor, of course, and from what one hears isn't what you'd call a monastic. But he's never done anything likely to cause trouble round here, and that's all we're interested in. What he does for his private amusement is no concern of ours.'

Paul thought of Bannerman's week of concerts and theatres, and smiled. The sergeant looked at him again. 'If you don't mind my saying so, sir,' he said, 'I still don't properly know what you think there is odd about Mr Bannerman. I should have said he was a very ordinary sort of gentleman, bar the fact that he's got plenty of money and never got married, which makes him different from most of us, in all conscience.'

'Yes. I didn't mean only that, of course. But he sort of throws it at you rather. Not so much the gay bachelor coming it over the married man – that's common enough. It's the way he prides himself on having everything of the best – on having a highly educated taste and being able to indulge it. It's a sort of showing off that one expects more in the very young. And yet he doesn't strike one as immature, quite. I find the two things hard to reconcile. But I do know this. Wherever Mr Bannerman got his money, he'd be lost without it.'

'That may be. But we've no reason to think he doesn't come by it honestly, so let's hope he continues to enjoy it. At least you and Mrs Mycroft have had some share in the enjoyment, which is more than most can say. He doesn't do much entertaining, and that's a fact. Had you met him often, then, sir?'

'Before he asked us to dinner? No. It was the first time we'd met.'

'Must have quite taken to you to ask you like that.'

'You're wondering whether he had any special reason for asking us? I know. My wife and I wondered the same thing. We came to the conclusion that we were, more than most of the visitors – well, people he'd think it worth showing off to, if you like. No, that's a bit hard. Let's say he thought we'd appreciate his good things more than most of them. He likes people to appreciate them, do you see, and he doesn't want to have people there who won't. I know it sounds odd, but then I told you – I think he is odd in that sort of way. Do you see what I mean?'

'I think so, pretty well. Of course, it isn't the kind of thing we get to see. So far as we're concerned, he's just what I said – a respectable sort of man with money to spend, who buys the place after the war – for a pretty steep price, by all accounts – and then learns the job and minds his own business a bit more than most.'

'He hadn't been a farmer before?'

'That I can't say. All I know is, he didn't seem to know much about it when he first come. But there was many took a fancy for farming after the war, and at least Mr Bannerman could afford to learn by making mistakes. It was the men with no money behind them after they'd bought the place that got into trouble. So there he still is and as I say probably doing quite well now. But he spends more than he makes on Bartenny, or so I'm told.'

'If he lives on the scale we saw,' said Paul, 'he certainly does. But don't think I'm against him. I admire a man who does things as well as that. I just can't make him out, that's all. Has he many friends round here? You say he doesn't entertain much.'

'I don't know that he has. As I say, he keeps himself to himself and doesn't go off the place much. But he does whatever's expected of him, and on the whole he's well liked.'

'The sergeant won't hear a word against Bannerman,' he told Mary later. 'Very respectable gentleman, even if he does keep himself to himself more than most.'

'That must be annoying for you. I don't know what you've got on him, but you start sniffing almost audibly when you get anywhere near him. All I've got against him is that he seems liable to spoil your holiday. But I admit he's an odd one. What does he do when there's no one about?'

'Like the tree in the quad? I know exactly what you mean. One gets the feeling that he exists – or at least the chap one knows exists – entirely in the eyes of other people. When the eyes aren't seeing him he must either virtually cease to exist or be somebody else. I mean, he can't just play with his treasures and wonder who he can show them to next. Or does he?'

'It's his smile I worry about. What does he do with it between-whiles?'

'When Miss Merrion has ceased to do for him and Ah Wong has packed up for the night? I know. Does he smile over his farm accounts or does he sit in that marvellous

116

west window and smile at the Carstone light?'

'Or doesn't he smile at all, don't you see? That's what worries me.'

'You know, there are quite a lot of people who live alone.'

'I know that. But with most of them you can imagine them doing it without any particular difficulty. I can't see him at all. And don't think I want to go and hold his hand. There's a bit of that, of course – that's probably why Cathie and I feel sorry for him. But in my heart of hearts I'm pretty certain he doesn't want it held. It's just that – I don't know – he isn't real enough to maintain an independent existence. Or something like that.'

'Another hollow man? There are too many of them round here. Could he have taken up with Millie, do you think? I'd have thought she wasn't his type at all, but perhaps I'm really thinking of Miss Merrion. Obviously Millie and Miss Merrion are pretty wildly different. But if Miss Merrion is one of his treasures, Millie might have been what he really needed – warmth and a general letting down of the hair and no questions asked.'

'And nothing to pay.'

'But he likes paying.'

'For his treasures, yes. Those are his conscious pleasures, that he has to smile at.'

'And Millie was every man's subconscious, demanding only the idiot-face of surrender?'

'That's it, more or less.'

'I wonder. That's a new picture of Millie, getting near Charles's, but definitely different. Aren't we building this thing up a bit? We don't even know he knew her, and he says he didn't. And even if he did know her, there still seems no reason why he should have pushed her into the sea. He didn't even have a wife to consider.'

117

Mary said, 'So far as Bannerman's concerned, you can rule out the *crime passionnel*. *Passion* isn't his strong suit. I wouldn't altogether rule out your picture of Millie as his sort of escape from the discipline of self-dramatisation. The immature streak, do you see? He might need someone he could bury his head in. But in general his love-life would be more of a piece with his treasure hunting and pretty closely calculated. Other people's wives are always, surely, a potential source of trouble. And he'd tend to keep trouble out of his love life as carefully as he keeps rain out of his roof.'

'Yes. That rather ties up with something the sergeant said. He said Bannerman was no monastic, but didn't do anything that might cause trouble locally and so be of interest to the police. Not that one would think of Millie as a source of that sort of trouble. You'd think she was as trouble-free as the latest dish-washer.'

'I know that. We were talking of reasons why he might have wanted to get rid of her – always supposing he was having an affair with her. And the point is, there wouldn't be any. He might have been the man she went to meet. After all, there he is, on Bartenny. But I can't see him, even so, as a likely murderer.'

'In fact, we have been, as I thought, building the thing up. It's perfectly obvious that to the ordinary observer – the sergeant, for instance – Bannerman is nowhere as a suspect. And so far as I'm concerned – well, I'm still a bit interested in Bannerman, but I don't see where Millie comes into it. I'm sorry about my audible sniffing. Very unprofessional. It was a queer party yesterday, wasn't it?'

'I think Cathie was right – we shouldn't have taken the children. They enjoyed themselves, but I wish we hadn't.'

'Actually we couldn't help ourselves. We were stuck without Susan, do you remember?'

'Could that really have been her out with Cardew, do you think – if it was Cardew?'

'I don't know. Bannerman wasn't holding out on us. He genuinely couldn't see, for all his special glasses. And anyway, he probably doesn't know her by sight. It would be interesting if it was. I said the Fraynes had a shock in store for them.'

'Would they know, do you think, if it was her?'

'It's difficult to say. Mrs Frayne wouldn't know that Cardew existed anyway. Frayne might persuade himself that it was the lobsters Susan was interested in. He says she's very young for her age and likes young company.'

Mary said, 'It depends how young.' Her tone was slightly acid.

'Cheer up,' said Paul. 'It was probably only a mermaid.'

Later, in the Lanting call-box, he said, 'I don't think so, but it might be worth Barlow's coming down. He doesn't fit the general picture badly, and he's certainly a bit of a mystery. But I can't see a sign of what you're looking for. Anyway, I'll keep an eye open.'

Outside the box he stopped, surveyed the empty car-park and said aloud, 'That's all very well. But what about Millie?'

CHAPTER THIRTEEN

'Take in the foresail a bit, will you,' said Dawson. 'I want to make her point a bit higher if I can.' The boat heeled gently and slid silently through the water into the mild breeze that blew up river from Skittle Hill.

Paul said, 'It was nice of you to let me come.'

'Glad to have you. I don't really care for sailing single-handed.'

'I'm no expert, as you know. But it doesn't look as if

119

conditions were going to be very demanding.'

'God, no. Why don't you take her yourself presently?'

'To be honest, I'd much rather not. I'm perfectly happy as I am. It's a sweet morning, and I enjoy merely going for a sail.'

They sat amicably side by side, and Paul considered surreptitiously the bronzed profile beside him. Like many enthusiasts, he thought, Dawson was much more acceptable in the practice of his passion than when talking about it. The passion was genuine enough. It was an escape, of course; but he could think of many worse ways of escaping and many people with less to escape from. Also, he was surprised to find, but still found, a pleasure in according Dawson a justifiable authority instead of humouring his weakness. He would have hated crewing for Frayne.

'Let's go about,' said Dawson. 'Are you ready?'

'Ready,' said Paul.

The boat went round in a smooth rush without perceptibly losing way and they settled themselves in their new places. Dawson said, 'I'm afraid I've been a bit under the weather lately.'

'Yes.' Paul wondered how much he remembered of their conversation in the room next to Charles's bar.

'Don't worry. I won't drown you.'

'I didn't think you would. Anyway, even if I look superficially more like a golfer than a sailor, I have in fact got a life-jacket on.' He turned and looked at Dawson. 'I'm sorry,' he said, 'I didn't—'

'I didn't say anything.' Dawson was watching the head of his sail. The eyes were puckered, as Paul had seen him pucker them when he talked sailing in the bar. The leathery, mobile mouth was sucked in, and there were hard lines, which he had never seen before, drawn down from the corners of the too prominent nose. It was not a good

120

face, but it had, at moments, a kind of obstinate tenacity. He flicked his eyes sideways suddenly at Paul. 'You don't take your sailing too seriously, do you?' he said.

'I don't take it seriously at all. As I say, I like just going for a sail. I know just enough to get my kind of pleasure out of it, and I avoid very carefully putting myself in circumstances where I might need to know more. I do get very great pleasure, in fact, and at least I avoid being a nuisance to other people. Whatever I think about sailing, I assure you I take the sea very seriously indeed.'

Dawson nodded. 'I never got to sea,' he said. 'I mean, not properly. I always wanted to, but it didn't work out. Not even in the war. I saw myself commanding a corvette, and they put me in the Pay Corps. Better qualified, I suppose. And of course now I can't get away. But something about twelve tons would be nice, wouldn't it? You could live on it and go anywhere within reason.'

Paul said, 'Not really my kind of life. I can see the beauty of it, but I'd miss things.'

'You're lucky. I can't think of anything I'd miss.' He said it almost jovially, with the dreadful determined cheerfulness of the hopelessly crippled.

'Would you sail your twelve-tonner single-handed?' said Paul.

'Alone? God, no. But the company would have to be right. You know. Something beautiful and cheerful and fond of the sea. And preferably something that could be paid off at the port of arrival.'

'You're asking a lot,' said Paul.

'Am I? I don't think so.' He took his eye off the peak and looked closely at Paul. 'Am I being offensive?' he said. 'You're a happily married man, whatever that means. Sorry if I'm not observing the decencies. That's the worst of being sober.'

Paul smiled resolutely and shook his head. 'You won't worry me,' he said. 'You must find the decencies come expensive.'

For a moment Dawson said nothing. Then he said, 'I don't want to get too close under Skittle. I'm going to go round and run up river for a bit. All right?'

The breeze died out of their faces, and in the sudden deceptive hush as the boat went off the wind Dawson laughed. 'I don't have to be drunk all the time,' he said. 'Only when the heat is on to an unbearable extent. There was a series of monumental rows last week. I suppose you know. Everyone did. They were largely conducted in public. It started over Millie Trent, as a matter of fact.' He laughed again. 'You'd think that when poor Millie was drowned things would ease up. I mean, it doesn't seem reasonable to keep up a hate for a woman that's dead. But you'd be surprised. I don't know what you'd do, but I just reach for the bottle. I've been on it more or less ever since.'

Paul thought very carefully. Then he said, 'I knew there had been rows, yes. And I saw you were putting it away pretty solidly. It's difficult to tell how things are from outside.'

'Bloody exhibition. Sort of wild beast show. And all over poor old Millie. Well, you knew Millie. She was a sweetie all right, but she wasn't a serious threat to home and hearth.'

'I didn't, as a matter of fact. I'd just about met her and seen her around.'

'And heard them talking about her?'

'And that, too, yes.'

'And what was your impression?'

'Well, I'd say one of cheerful and big-hearted promiscuity.'

122

'But you never put your belief to the test – being, as I say, a happily married man?'

'No. But wait a minute. I lay no claim to more than mortal virtue. It's just that – well, that sort of woman – or at any rate the sort of woman I thought Millie was – sets up a resistance in me. Something gets in the way mentally. One's pride, or one's sense of humour, or something – I don't know.'

'You like them harder to get?'

'I don't like that way of putting it. But at least it doesn't make me sound too much of a cold-boiled prig. And I don't really think I am one. In fact, I'm damned sure I'm not. I have in my time subsequently regretted this particular reaction. I've wondered what could have come over me. But it had come over me, nevertheless.'

'I'm going to gybe. But it will hardly wake the baby.' The boom swung over with a gentle thud and they settled comfortably on their new course.

'I like this kind of sailing,' said Paul. 'Do you mind if I trail my hand in the water? I'm almost too hot.'

'You can take off your shoes and paddle if you like. I'm not particular so long as you don't upset the boat.'

'Anyway, without going further into the mental impediments to my sex-life, what it comes to is that I never took any steps to confirm the impression I had of Millie Trent. It may have been wrong.'

'I wouldn't say so. But you see what I mean. That isn't the sort of thing for a wife to raise hell over. Not if she's wise. It's as casual as an occasional booze-up. And much cheaper, if it's the housekeeping she's worried about. And I think half the time it is.'

'Whereas if she does raise hell and you, as you say, reach for the bottle, it sets the housekeeping back no end?'

'That's right. It does, in fact.'

123

'Well, it's one way of looking at matrimony.'

Dawson looked at him. His eyes were puckered into brown slots and his rubbery smile was wide. Paul noticed with a faint surprise that his teeth were white and perfectly kept.

'Not noble, is it?' he said. 'All right, I grant you it's not noble. But there have got to be some terms. There's got to be a basis, wherever you put it. Would you say old Trent was a sadder bugger than I am? I mean, before Millie was drowned.'

For a moment Paul wrestled with his honesty. Then he said, 'No. No, as a matter of fact I don't think he was.'

'Well there you are then. As I say, it's a matter of the terms you settle for. We can't all be happily married men.' His invisible eyes shifted over Paul's shoulder. 'Look at old Frayne over there,' he said. 'Trying to make his boat go faster than the wind. He'd like a Force Six breeze, so that he can shout orders to his pretty Pam. It's not so easy to act young in a near calm. One may even have to make conversation to one's crew.' He grinned at Paul again.

'Don't mind me. I've come out for the sail.'

'I know, I know. I wasn't really meaning you. But look at Frayne, now. What terms has he settled for? He's married to an ornamental little iceberg that doesn't dare thaw a little for fear it melts altogether. So he totes around a pretty piece the same age as his daughter, who believe me doesn't give him anything he ought to get from his wife. I know Pam. She's a nice kid, and tough. He may lay an almost fatherly hand on her arm occasionally, but he doesn't lay it anywhere else, shorts or no shorts. Perhaps he doesn't want to. I wouldn't know. But what does he get out of it? He gets something, or why doesn't he take that daughter of his instead of leaving her to run loose? I know he says Pam's the better sailor. She may be a little,

124

but don't tell me it's the sailing he's really thinking of. If Susan was the better sailor, he'd still take Pam. And his wife would still let him. There's a funny basis there somewhere, don't you think?'

Paul said, 'I agree with you about what he doesn't get out of it. If he was thinking of laying an almost fatherly hand here and there, it wouldn't be a Force Six breeze he'd be wanting. I don't think he wants much more than to flex his muscles and assure himself he's as young as he feels. He is happy, I think, in his way. Not my way, of course, nor, I imagine, yours. He's the boyish type, isn't he?'

Dawson laughed. 'Boyish is good,' he said. 'Well, I suppose that's one way of putting it. I've heard it called other things, but boyish will do. So long as his wife doesn't mind. Which of course she doesn't, so long as he puts her cushions where she wants them and gets up in the night to give her her medicine. If those are the terms they've settled on, good luck to them. I agree he's not unhappy, exactly. As you say, it isn't my idea of happiness, but I wouldn't set myself up as an authority on married bliss.'

He looked astern and sniffed. 'This is going to die out altogether if we're not careful. I think we'd better make for home, unless you want to finish rowing.'

'Not me,' said Paul. 'I may be a poor sailor, but I'm an even worse waterman. I've enjoyed it. But let's get home by all means. Or at any rate, let's try.'

Nearly three hours later Paul came out of the telephone box and listened. From the far end of the hall there came to him, through shut doors, the confused noise of the Carrack Hotel at lunch. He put his head round the door of the bar. It was empty. Charles was polishing glasses with scholarly intensity. Paul pushed open the door and walked in. He said, 'I've been sailing with Dawson.'

125

Charles put down the glass he was polishing and looked at him. 'Have you now?' he said. With no one else in the bar, Paul noticed, the interview was to be on the unprofessional, or sand dunes, basis. 'Did he ask you or you him?'

'He me. The wind almost died on us. We ghosted home on what was left of it against quite a bit of tide. It was nicely done, I must say. He can certainly sail that boat of his. But it took a long time, even so. I have just been assuring my wife that I have survived the perils of the voyage and am come safe to land. Do you keep anything to eat here?'

Charles produced a plate of savoury biscuits. 'That's the best I can do, I'm afraid. What did Dawson have to say to you all this time?'

'During the whole return journey, nothing but sailing orders. He was completely absorbed and in the circumstances good company. Earlier he had given a fairly elaborate exposition of the smoke-room gent. At least, that's how he started.'

'Did he tell you his story about the museum attendant and the American tourist?'

'No. Should he have?'

'I should have thought so.'

'No, he talked about his wife, himself and Millie Trent, after first pointing out that he had been drunk for some time but was now sober. Later he got on to matrimonial relations generally. That was pretty raw stuff, but I should say unpremeditated and in its depressing way not unintelligent. He is not a nice man, but at least he has the grace to know how nasty he is. He also has, I suppose, in the exercise of the same judgment, a considerable insight into the nastiness of others.'

'He was out to shock,' said Charles.

'In a way, yes. To begin with, anyhow. Later he was merely intrinsically shocking.'

'What do you think he wanted you to derive from the conversation? And what in fact did you derive?'

Paul thought. 'He didn't refer at all to the time he talked to me in that room next door. Either he has forgotten about it or he wants me to think he has.'

'There is another possibility. He may have a confused recollection of talking to you and be wondering what the hell he said.'

'Yes, that's also possible. For what it's worth, I rather fancy that he hasn't forgotten the conversation, not completely anyhow, and is concerned to offset whatever impression it may have made on me. He was certainly at pains to impress on me the difference between Dawson drunk and Dawson sober, with the fairly clear implication that the second, though nastier, was the more reliable of the two.'

'In what respects, in fact, did what he said today differ from what he said the first time?'

'I think mainly in the picture that emerged of Millie Trent and of his relations with her – or rather, his attitude to her. Dawson sober, in his nastiness, sees her – well, I'm afraid rather as I saw her myself. The cheerful tart, good for a casual coupling, but unlikely to be of any permanent significance to anybody, and therefore, by Dawson sober's standards, nothing for a wife to complain about, let alone drive her husband to drink over. To Dawson drunk she had been, I should say, a good deal more than this. I'm not even sure, now I come to think of it, she had been a tart at all. You see the difficulty? Dawson drunk is on the whole the more sympathetic character of the two. Yet Dawson sober would disclaim Dawson drunk. No *veritas,* for him, in Dawson's *vino.* I find that odd.'

127

'I agree. Dr Jekyll talking hard in the cold light of morning to blur the overnight features of Mr Hyde – that's fairly familiar. It never works, not so far as I am concerned, but that doesn't stop Dr Jekyll talking. But to have Mr Hyde grinning at you over breakfast about something that ass Jekyll said last night – that's certainly uncommon. I wasn't in on either conversation, but to me it stinks.'

'Yes, but why do it? When you say it stinks, what you mean is that you don't think Mr Hyde is wholly genuine. Despite the improbability of a man's deliberately blackguarding himself, you believe he is nicer than he says he is. But you've still got to explain why he is blackguarding himself. Dr Jekyll may be more convincingly identifiable as the man you're talking to, but he still has, if I may dare to say so, something to hide. The question is, what?'

'Something, obviously, to do with Millie. His relations with his wife bear no concealment and will hardly bear exaggeration.'

'You're seen them before. Have they always been as bad as this?'

Charles considered this. 'So far as I am concerned,' he said, 'Mrs Dawson would always have driven me to drink, ever since I've known her. And I don't think her behaviour to him has changed. What has changed is his reaction.'

'His being, in fact and at last, driven to drink?'

'If you like, yes.'

'If it was her that drove him,' said Paul.

The door swung open suddenly and Colonel Frayne came in. He said, 'Hullo, Mycroft. Charles, give me a nice gin quickly, and I'll see if they can find me any lunch. We got completely becalmed. Is Dawson back?'

'Oh yes,' said Paul, 'we got in some time ago.'

'You were with him, were you? How did you get in?'

'Sailed,' said Paul.

Colonel Frayne shook his head. 'Don't believe it,' he said. 'Dawson must have got a concealed motor. Look, I've been meaning to ask you. You and your wife have been so good to Susan lately. We were wondering whether you'd come and dine with us?'

'We'd love to. I'll ask Mary, of course, but I know she'd love it.'

'Good. What about tomorrow? Sue won't mind sitting in for you.'

'Tomorrow would be fine, if Susan's available.'

'Available?' said Colonel Frayne. 'Of course she'll be available. Why shouldn't she be?'

CHAPTER FOURTEEN

'You're always being asked to dinner, aren't you,' said Susan, 'and by the most unlikely people. I suppose one thing sort of leads to another. I've never known Daddy and Mummy invite anyone to dine with them – not down here, I mean. I'm sure it was your being invited by Mr Bannerman that put it into Daddy's head.'

'He said they wanted to thank us for being so good to you – lately,' said Paul. 'Rather a negative qualification, perhaps. Come on, Mary, or we shall be a good deal more than polite late.'

'It would be more to the point if I could invite you to something,' said Susan. 'I don't quite know what. Anyway,' she said as Mary appeared, 'have a good time and try to look as if the Carrack food is as good as Mr Bannerman's. I don't mind telling you it won't be, but then you'd hardly expect it. Be kind to Daddy, won't you?' she said to Paul.

'I'll do my best to spare his feelings,' said Paul. Susan waved and the car moved off.

'There's an uncertain conscience for you,' said Paul.

'Uncertain possibly,' said Mary, 'guilty, no. She gives me the impression of someone spoiling for a fight, but not at all clear who she is going to fight or why.'

'Time will show. But in any case I think I'm on her side. I could do with something pretty crude to drink before we start. I fancy this is an evening to be gone through rather than enjoyed. But it may well have its funny side.'

'It could be a riot. But if you feel unsafe we could stop at the pub and you could down something quick and stiff.'

'Nonsense. Let come what may. I fear neither the Fraynes' hospitality nor the Carrack food.'

'Well, remember what Sue said. Be kind to Daddy. That means, among other things, don't be too fierce with Mummy. She will get one of her heads, and then Daddy will be up with her half the night.'

'I won't be fierce with her, I promise. I will soothe and cosset her till she doesn't know her hair-bleach from her stomach-powder. What's her name, by the way? I've never heard it, I don't think. I hope it's something in character like Mrs Dawson's Agnes.'

'I'm trying to remember. I'm sure I've heard it. Something faint and sugary, it ought to be.'

'Ratafia? Or Sarsaparilla? That would be nice. Sarsaparilla Frayne is a poem in itself.'

'It will probably be something wildly unsuitable. But whatever it is, don't catch my eye when it emerges.'

Mrs Frayne said, 'Hul-*lo*,' and stretched out a little jewelled hand to them from the depths of her chair. Her feet were tucked up beside her and her head was on a cushion. Only her arm moved from the shoulder down, so that Paul, bending over her, was uncertain whether he ought to kiss her ring or feel her pulse. He settled for a slight squeeze of the cold, silky fingers, and her brow contracted slightly. He wondered what would have happened if he had grasped them firmly.

Colonel Frayne said to Mary, 'This is fun. It's so nice of you to come along.' He towered happily over his prostrate wife, like a St Bernard standing on trust over a plate of cold chicken. 'Her mother and I are so grateful for all the time you have given to Susan. She can't do much for her herself, you know, and it is so good for her to have young company.'

Paul took a breath, and Mary had the panic-stricken conviction that he was going to say, 'I'm so glad her mother and her father are pleased.' She said quickly, 'We've loved having her, and it's us that should be grateful. She's made herself tremendously useful.'

Colonel Frayne said, 'What can I get you to drink? They're not over-staffed here, and it's always quicker to collect them for oneself.'

'I'd like a gin and French, please.'

'Gin and French for the lady. You'd like a whisky and soda, Paul, as I should myself? Anything for you, my dear?' He bent anxiously over his wife. 'Have a small one, why not? It will do you good.'

Mrs Frayne looked up at him and held up a white finger and thumb very close together. 'Just a wee gin at the bottom of a dry ginger,' she said. '*Dry* ginger, please, and very little gin.'

Paul said, 'I'll come and help you carry them.'

Colonel Frayne said, 'Don't bother, old chap,' but Paul followed him into the bar.

'Good evening, Colonel Frayne. Good evening, Mr Mycroft,' said Charles. 'What can I get you?'

'Two nice whiskies and sodas, please,' said Colonel

131

Frayne. 'And a gin and French. And for Mrs Frayne a gin and dry ginger.' He looked firmly at Charles.

Charles repeated the order in a professional sing-song and swung into action. Colonel Frayne turned his back on the bar and said to Paul, 'Place not as full as it was. Getting near the end of the season.'

'I suppose it is. We've only got another week.' He watched over Colonel Frayne's shoulder and saw Charles draw two double whiskies, a single gin and a double gin. He said, 'Not—' and checked. The dry ginger fell modestly on to the double gin, barely colouring it. 'Not,' said Paul, 'that you'd think so from the weather. It's as fine as it's been all the summer.'

'Wonderful,' said Colonel Frayne absently, 'it's been wonderful. Ah.' He swung round as Charles put the glasses on the bar. 'You take the whiskies, will you, Paul? I'll see to the others.' They processed back. Mrs Frayne did not seem to have moved a muscle since they left.

Mary said to Paul, 'I've been telling Mrs Frayne how useful Susan's been to us. Especially this last week.' she added.

'Have you?' said Paul. 'Indeed, yes. I'm sure you underestimate that daughter of yours, Mrs Frayne.'

Mrs Frayne said, 'So long as the girl's happy and not being a nuisance to you.' She did not, Paul noticed, say either gel or gairl. Her voice was as small as the rest of her, but her accent was precise and completely unaffected.

'Oh yes,' said Paul, 'she's happy all right.'

'Thanks to you largely, I'm sure,' said Colonel Frayne. 'Well, good health.'

Mrs Frayne lifted her glass with a sort of placid resignation and sipped. She did not bat an eye. This, no doubt, was what her wee gins always tasted like.

People passed to and fro, with or without glasses in their

hands. They nodded or said good evening to each other. The noise from the bar increased, and Paul thought he could hear the voice of Dawson in his role of Jolly Jack. He looked round for Agnes, but could not see her.

Mrs Frayne said, 'It always gets so terribly noisy at this time.' She lifted a brow of wrinkled alabaster, and Paul half expected Colonel Frayne to bustle round asking everyone to be a little quieter, please. Instead he said, 'Never mind, my dear. They'll be putting on dinner soon. It's less noisy here than in the bar.'

On such an evening, not many evenings ago, Major Trent had been asking where Millie was, and everyone was talking about it, surreptitiously, with glances over their shoulders. At just this time, and in the middle of this clamour, Dawson had come into the bar with the devil at his elbow and begun systematically on the drinking bout from which he had only lately recovered.

' "Waal" ' said Dawson's voice in the bar. He spoke in a burlesque American accent. ' "Waal," she said, "that sure is the cutest museum piece I ever saw." ' There was a roar of laughter and some shrill feminine cries of protest.

A man in a waisted reefer jacket with badges on the brass buttons pushed past Paul, spilling a little of his whisky. He turned and thrust a sunburnt face into Paul's. 'I say, old boy,' he said, 'terribly sorry. Let me get you another.'

'Nonsense,' said Paul, 'I didn't lose much.' The man was already gone.

Colonel Frayne stood very straight with a wary smile on his face. 'So sorry,' he said. 'We get a few queer ones at times, you know, even here.'

Paul gave him a man-of-the-world smile and said, 'Get them everywhere.' He drank the rest of his whisky quickly before another queer one came along.

Colonel Frayne looked at his watch. 'Time for another before we eat,' he said. 'Let me get you one.' Paul said, 'Thanks,' and he took the glasses and went.

'It's rather gay here,' said Mary to Mrs Frayne. 'We're not used to this excitement.'

Mrs Frayne smiled despairingly and shrank back into her chair. Her wee gin was nearly finished.

Millie would have loved this, thought Paul. She would not have added to the noise herself much, but she would have been up at the bar, perched on a high stool with all her curves breath-takingly arranged, in one of those shiny house-coat things he had last seen hanging in the cupboard of Room 23, still smelling of her, with the salt-stained life-jacket underneath their skirts. Only on the evening he was thinking of she had been lolloping in the sea, somewhere in the tide run between Bartenny and Lanting, with her jersey sodden and her eyes staring blindly at the already darkening sky.

Colonel Frayne said, 'Here we are,' at his elbow. 'Brought 'em back intact, anyhow.' He smiled his watchful, Boy-Scout smile. 'Thanks,' said Paul again.

'Mrs Mycroft,' said Colonel Frayne, 'what about you? One more before we eat?' She shook her head in the tumult and showed him her glass still half-full. Mrs Frayne seemed to have her eyes shut.

Mrs Dawson came down the stairs in a rust-coloured frock that hung straight on her. She walked to the door of the bar and looked in. There was another shout of laughter and a woman's voice said ecstatically, 'Oh, that's *awful*.' Agnes turned and went through a door on the other side of the hall marked Writing Room on a polished brass plate. She looked venomous.

Paul caught Colonel Frayne's eye and saw that he had seen her too. He shrugged slightly, but his expression was

134

calculatedly neutral.

The gong sounded from the end of the hall. It was a brassy cheerful sound, crying its wares with confidence. Paul remembered the five strokes of doom that had summoned them to that wonderful meal in the candle-lit western room on Bartenny. He wondered whether Bannerman was summoned every evening by five strokes of the bell. Perhaps Ah Wong, if it had been Ah Wong, could not find the time for bell ringing when she had all the cooking to do herself.

He found Mrs Frayne uncoiling herself effortlessly while her husband hovered over her. Mary was already standing beside him. Someone behind him said, 'Well, what about a spot of food?' It was so like Charles's imitation that he half expected to see that noble head making for the dining-room.

Colonel Frayne said, 'All set?' Paul finished his whisky quickly and put the glass down on a copy of the *Yachting World* already ringed from similar emergencies. They moved off, part of a drifting column of bodies, towards a door at the far end of the hall.

At the door Colonel Frayne said, 'Our usual place, I think, but they've given us a larger table.' Mrs Frayne, poised and erect for all her visible suffering, nodded and led Mary forward. It was quieter here, and Paul suddenly realised that conversation would be necessary.

He said, 'They've made an awfully pleasant room of this, haven't they?'

Mrs Frayne looked wonderingly round the shining cream-coloured walls. She said, 'They've painted it, I think.' They settled in their places.

Colonel Frayne said, 'Oh, they've done a lot this last year or two. Smartened it all up no end. It was always very comfortable, you know, even when we first came here,

135

but nothing terribly smart. It's the sailing people they cater for. A lot of us come here every year.'

They started on their tinned grapefruit. The room was filling up now. The staff was anything from local wives working part-time to whole-time, but seasonal, Mediterranean males. They all wore white coats and bustled about cheerfully. The atmosphere was holiday and the idiom middleclass, so that everybody, even what Colonel Frayne called the queer ones, seemed to be just home from the same boarding school. Colonel Frayne, obviously, was already beginning to have doubts, as the level of money rose and the proportion of queer ones rose with it. He came, of course only for the sailing, but even on the river things must be changing. Mrs Frayne was there, against all the odds, because in this as in some other things she let her husband do what he wanted. Paul doubted whether she really minded much, or even noticed, where they went for their holidays. She carried her own small island of consciousness about with her, and it was powerfully fenced.

'—and there was Cathleen,' Mary was saying, 'with the book marked and Sue's supper laid, all set for a cosy, girl-to-girl evening even before Sue got there. And she doesn't take to people too easily as a rule.'

'You've got to hand it to Dawson,' said Colonel Frayne, 'he's a wonderful light-weather sailor. We must both have turned for home at much the same time yesterday, and you were in a good three-quarters of an hour before I was.'

'He certainly concentrates,' said Paul. 'Never said a word all the way home except to tell me what to do. It suited me, of course. Nothing I like better.'

'He was lucky in his crew,' said Colonel Frayne. 'I felt a bit guilty about young Pam, I must say. It's all right in a good sailing breeze when there's plenty for them to do, but the young things are apt to get bored in a calm, and it upsets one's judgment. There he is now, as a matter of fact.' Paul heard chairs drawn out over his left shoulder. Somewhere over to his right a gurgling feminine voice said, 'Oh, that's *lovely.*' It was the same voice that had said it was awful in the bar. Paul looked. She was very pretty, but her chin fell away too much when she smiled, which she did nearly all the time. She had probably succeeded to Millie's mantle for the rest of the season, but seemed hardly qualified for it. This was the time, when everybody was well settled and had got their heads temporarily out of their plates, that Millie would have staged her entrance. He could almost see Colonel Frayne's head snap back and his cautious mouth harden down from the corners of the nostrils as he watched her hips move between the tables. Did all the male conversation die out, he wondered, or did it waver and continue at random until she sat down? Major Trent, economical in movement and with his eyes hooded, came after her.

'What colour were you thinking of, then?' said Dawson.

'I thought a kind of cerise for the lounge,' said Agnes, 'and something a bit brighter for the curtains.'

'That sounds all right. Water?'

'No thanks.'

'To tell you the truth,' said Colonel Frayne, 'I've been wondering at times whether we should go on coming down here. I like the sailing, of course, and we have friends here. There are a lot of advantages in coming to the same place every year. But I don't think Susan has enjoyed it much this year, and she ought to be finding company nearer her own age. Mind you, I don't mind her being a bit young for her age. Rather that than the other way round. But it's not good for her to be too much on her own, and her mother isn't up to doing much with her.'

137

Paul said, 'They are a responsibility. You'll be glad when she's a bit older and can take herself off your hands completely.'

'That's right. It's got to come, of course. I don't believe in keeping them tied. But of course Susan's young yet, you know. Only left school this year.'

'Or we might put the blue upstairs,' said Agnes.

'Yes, that would be all right.' There was a pause.

'Do you know we haven't got a blue? I suppose you've never noticed?'

'Oh, haven't we? I must have been thinking—'

'I know what you were thinking about all right. Not about what I was saying, that's certain. It's like having meals with a dummy. Only a dummy doesn't smell of drink.'

'I can't think what they put in these puddings,' said Mrs Frayne. 'They always seem to have such a strange taste. I don't expect they do one any harm, but they are curious.'

'It's the whale-blubber,' said Paul. Mrs Frayne opened her eyes wide, her spoon half-way to her mouth 'It's in the ice-cream mix, I'm told, and of course they use ice-cream in nearly all these puddings now. It's very useful in soufflés and light things – doesn't need any beating. But you do get the taste a bit, I know. It's all right when it's frozen, you see. In point of fact I'm told half the people who eat them never really taste these mass-produced ice-creams at all. Have to gulp them down, most of them, because of their teeth. But if you'd ever eaten some thawed out, you'd know all right. Mind you, you're perfectly right – it's absolutely harmless, and I believe extremely nourishing. But one does just get that taste at times.' Mrs Frayne put her spoon down.

Colonel Frayne said, 'Don't you believe it, Tanny, Paul's

only pulling your leg.' But there was a hint of panic in his voice.

'You've lost the Carrack three seasonal bookings,' said Mary in the car. 'They'll never come again, not with whale-blubber in the puddings.'

'They won't anyhow, unless I'm very much mistaken. What in the world do you suppose Tanny is short for? Titanic? Titania? Do you think I dare ask Susan?'

Susan was in her usual chair. Everything was quiet. She did not seem to have been reading. She got up and faced them as they came in from the verandah. She said, 'Oh, hullo. Was it all right?'

Paul said, 'If you mean what I think you mean, yes, as a matter of fact it was. But I think it's time we had a talk, don't you?'

Mary said, 'Oh Paul, it's late now. Sue ought to get back.'

'Sit down, Sue,' said Paul.

CHAPTER FIFTEEN

Susan sat down, very straight and watchful, on the edge of a chair. Paul plumped himself in the big chair she had just left. He said, 'Your parents think you've been with us almost continuously this past week. In fact, as you know, we've hardly seen you. It wouldn't be any of my business, but you've put both Mary and me in a pretty false position with your parents. Wisely or unwisely, we neither of us blew the gaff this evening. But I think we're entitled to an explanation.'

'I didn't ask you to tell lies for my sake,' said Susan. 'I didn't expect you would. That was your decision. I never would have asked you to, you know that.'

Paul sighed. 'Look,' he said, 'let's for goodness sake not over-dramatise this. On the other hand, let's not be too jesuitical. It's perfectly true you never asked us not to tell your parents you hadn't been here. But you know us pretty well by now. You were pretty certain, weren't you, that if the wires did get crossed we should come to you for an explanation before we told them. And so we have. I don't really think you can now sit back and throw the responsibility on us.'

Mary, who had been standing in the inner doorway, came into the room, shut the door behind her and sat down at the table. 'So far as I am concerned,' she said, 'I merely want to know and want if possible to help. I'm not standing on my right to an explanation. But there is another thing. Whatever the rights or wrongs of what's happened, things can't go on as they have been. We may not feel called on to tell your parents that you haven't been here this last week, but now we know the position we're certainly not going even to let your parents think you're here when you're not. So either you've got to think up something else or you've got to have the thing out. I don't honestly recommend the first. And if the thing's coming out anyhow, I'm sure you'd better let us have it first.'

'It's already coming out,' said Paul. 'Dawson said something yesterday I didn't like the sound of, but I didn't want to press him for an explanation.'

'What did Mr Dawson say?' Susan was pale with anger.

'I forget exactly, but something about your being allowed to run loose, or some such phrase. At any rate, there was a clear implication that your parents didn't know what you were up to.'

'Damned old gossip.'

'So he may be, but he's not the only one. If he talks, the rest will.'

'It makes it all seem so shoddy, and it's not shoddy at all.'

Paul and Mary waited. 'Well,' said Paul, 'what isn't?'

'I've been out with Mike Cardew.'

There was a moment's silence. 'If it's any comfort to you,' said Paul, 'I'm neither surprised nor shocked, and Mary is probably consumed with jealousy. Was it really impossible to tell your parents?'

'Absolutely. In any case, the thing – just started, you know. I was down along the river, walking by myself because I was bored, and we met by chance. That was a couple of days after our trip. It was lovely seeing him again, and we talked, and I found I wasn't bored at all. He said he was going out to his pots in the afternoon and I said could I come. He said of course. There was nothing else to it. It was only when I got back to the hotel that I realised I couldn't tell Mummy and Daddy. They'd either have stopped me or made the whole thing stink. I didn't actually tell them I was coming here. I just let them assume it.'

'Yes. Well, all that's easy enough. And you've been seeing quite a good deal of him since?'

'Every day, pretty well. Whenever I could get away. He picks me up down near the river mouth.'

'Does he? Whose idea was that?'

'Oh, mine. I couldn't go off with Mike from the jetty, could I?'

'No. On the present basis I suppose not. What does Mike think about it?'

'I – I don't know. He hasn't said anything. I just asked him to meet me there and he said he would.'

'But he must see why. Doesn't it worry him?'

'I don't know, I tell you. We simply haven't talked about it. We never talk about anything on shore at all once we're

141

away. It's as though it didn't exist.'

Mary said, 'What do you talk about?'

Susan looked at her as if the question was a slightly un-
reasonable one. 'Well, about the job, of course – Mike's
job. The boat, the sea, the fish, the weather – all that. Mike
knows it all inside out. I've learnt a lot, but of course I've
scarcely started.'

'So what it comes to is this. You've made friends with
Mike Cardew. You help him, so far as you can, with his
job, you're interested in it and he's teaching you something
about it. You're – what? – seventeen?'

'Eighteen next month.'

'And how old do you suppose he is?'

'Mike's twenty-four. I asked him.'

Paul smiled. 'Relevant to his job, I suppose, just. All
right, now so far as I'm concerned, Mike Cardew being
the man I think he is, there's nothing wrong with all this
at all – so far. I can see possible future snags, but for the
moment it's all, literally and figuratively, plain sailing. The
big snag now is that your parents don't know about it,
and that you have deliberately kept it from them. It's not
so much the fact that they don't know – it's the fact that
you don't want them to. That's the fact you've got to concentrate on. You say they'd either stop you going or make
the whole thing stink. In either case, why?'

Susan thought. 'It's Daddy, really. He'd be frightfully
worried about it. Being a man, and really pretty fair-
minded, he'd know at once, if he met Mike, that there was
nothing against him as a person. But he'd still feel, in a
plaintive, wronged sort of way, that I ought to make
friends in my own class. He'd think I'd let the side down.
He might even say that. And the extraordinary thing is
that if I went out with someone like the Bellenger boy,
with his sports car and his London clothes, Daddy

142

wouldn't mind a bit, regardless of the fact that I'd be involved in practically a hand-to-hand struggle for my virtue at the first dark bend in the road.'

'Which I take it you're not with Mike?'

'Mike? Oh no.'

'Your father's not to know that, and it won't stop him worrying. It may not be reasonable, but the fact is that, Mike being the age and class he is, your father is going to think that if you go on seeing much of him, you'll be having an affair with him. The point is, will you?'

Susan shook her head. 'No,' she said in a rather small voice, 'oh no.'

Paul looked at her. 'Try again,' he said.

Susan managed a wan smile. 'I told you,' she said. 'He hasn't suggested it.'

'So you've already said. But supposing he did?'

Susan's mouth wobbled and her eyes seemed twice their normal size. 'I don't know,' she said. 'I love him so much I don't know what I'd do.' She looked from one to the other of them despairingly, and for a moment Paul saw a strong, incongruous likeness to her mother. 'I'm sorry,' she said. 'He's almost the only honest person I've ever met – Mike, and you two, and Millie Trent, and she's dead. That's all.' She sobbed suddenly, and Mary was at her side with one arm round her shoulders.

She said, 'Paul, I doubt if we can get much futher tonight, and I'm sure Sue ought to get back to the hotel.'

Paul said, 'There is one more thing. I'm sorry to grind on it rather, Sue, but I really do need to know. You say Mike Cardew has never – oh lor, aren't there any words for it not tainted with vulgarity?'

'Never made a pass at me? No, he never has.'

'All right, I accept that. Then what is the relationship on his side? I mean – well, to use a handy yardstick, has he kissed you?'

Susan shook her head. She seemed overcome with desolation. 'That simply isn't on the cards,' she said. 'I don't know what he thinks or feels privately. He doesn't wear his heart on his sleeve exactly, Mike. But so far as his behaviour goes, I'm the kid next door. Not the kid sister.' She looked at them hotly, and Paul in spite of himself found himself smiling. 'I think my company means quite a lot to him. I know he likes having me to talk to, and he finds me – oh, receptive, if you like. I like most of the things he likes, and if I'm interested I'm a quick learner. He likes me as a person all right. But whether he finds me attractive, God only knows. I don't.' She appealed to Mary. 'Don't you think he must, a little, to see as much of me as he does?'

Mary shook her head. 'No comment, my child,' she said. 'I simply don't know. I might know if I saw you together. I thought you were – well, on terms, in touch, *en rapport*, whatever the phrase is, on the day of our trip to the Tabernacles. But I admit it was you I was mostly thinking of. I was surprised to find you so much – I don't know, at home in a boat, perhaps. And I was curiously touched when he gave you the fish. But what it all meant to him I don't pretend to know. As you say, he doesn't throw his feelings around exactly.'

Paul got up. 'Come on,' he said. 'I'll run you back. You're your own mistress, but if I were you I'd not go out with Mike Cardew – tomorrow, anyhow – to give the hotel time to simmer down. As for the future – look, do you mind if I speak to him?'

Susan, on her way to the door, stopped short. 'What about?' she said.

'You, generally. More specifically, his relations with you.'

144

'But you mustn't – Promise you won't do anything to stop him seeing me?'

'I couldn't do that even if I wanted to. I haven't the least ground for doing so, or any right to ask it, still less demand it. But I should be much happier in my own mind if I had had a talk with him, and I shall if I get the chance. But I promise you that whatever, as the result of that conversation, I think ought to be done, I won't do a thing until I've talked to you about it.'

Susan nodded. 'That's fair enough,' she said. 'Anyhow, I can't prevent you, can I?'

'Not really,' said Paul, 'no. Do tell me, why does your father call your mother Tanny?'

'Oh that? It's short, sort of. She was christened Violet Annie, which doesn't suit her much. Tanny does rather, I think. Or perhaps I've just got used to it. But not Violet Annie.'

'Not anything Annie,' said Paul. 'Come on.'

CHAPTER SIXTEEN

'Say what you like about Pelant,' said Paul, 'it isn't oldy worldy. Look at this.' The stone cottage had its woodwork painted bright blue with polished brass on the door. A blue board facing the road said 'Mother Picton's Pantry.' The windows had been knocked out to three times their proper size and showed tables with chrome legs and plastic tops.

The street dropped sharply between the tourist attractions until they were diverted into a car-park which seemed to have been dynamited casually out of the side of the cliff. They reached the harbour on foot. The boats moored

145

inside the bow-headed jetty were working boats with a handful of cruising yachts. Beyond the narrow mouth the cliffs fell back abruptly, taking at their base the ground swell of the open sea. There were no beaches and no flat stretches of sheltered water for the convenience of the dinghy sailor. Cainport had prettified its ruggedness for the summer visitor, but the process could not be carried beyond the harbour mouth.

'It isn't as nice as Mr Cardew's boat,' said Cathleen. 'It's bigger, but it's older and dirtier.'

'So's the fisherman,' said Mary. 'Oh dear.'

Paul said, 'Never mind. She's safe and roomy, and you can see a new bit of coast. What's the good of going to sea if you can't explore? Good afternoon, Mr Menloe. We're on time, I think.'

Mr Menloe raised a mahogany face and lowered it again, so that they were not sure whether he was giving them a quick look-over or an economical nod. He said, 'Best get them in quick. Tide won't hold.' His voice was husky. He turned and spat with a hollow thudding noise into the oily waters of the harbour behind him.

For a moment the whole family hung back. Then the sun, which had been cloud-covered since morning, suddenly poured itself into the hollow of Cainport harbour, and they saw Mr Menloe and his dubious boat floating on liquid emerald at the bottom of corn-coloured steps. Jennifer said, 'Golly!' and they all surged forward. The boat rang as solid and hollow as a pontoon as they jumped successively aboard. Mr Menloe said, 'Cast off forward, do you mind, sir?' and started his engine. They were nosing out between the harbour arms before they had chosen their places or stowed their gear. But Mr Menloe was astern and the view ahead was breath-taking. The children clustered excitedly in the bows. Paul, his responsibilities temporarily discharged, relaxed and took stock.

Cainport had not bothered to advertise itself to seaward. It clung to its cleft in the rock in a falling series of primeval greys and buffs that brought up short on the solid horizontal line of the harbour. They had barely left it, and already, Paul noticed, it was extraordinarily invisible. The water was dark under them, and they began to ride the swell in a long rocking motion that was convincing and not unpleasant. Ahead, the towering coastline stretched away, eastward until it disappeared into the still receding cloud, westward until it ended in the great hump, unmistakable even at this distance, of Bartenny Head.

He wondered what the mileage was and tried to recall the look of the map. He turned to ask Mr Menloe, but his intention spent itself on the uninviting mahogany mask, and he turned seawards again.

There was a power boat of some sort coming in, and he felt Mr Menloe alter course slightly to pass her. The sun had gone in again, and the swell seemed a little steeper. He looked at Mary. She was smiling bravely, but had a watchful eye on the children. He caught her eye across Mr Menloe's unchanging forward glare. He said, 'Can't have perfection twice. They going to be all right?'

She nodded. 'I think so. Jennifer's the one to watch. Seems a pity, all the same.'

'It couldn't be helped. It had to be today, and I'm not seeing him till tomorrow.'

'I know. Don't worry. If only the sun comes out this may surprise us yet.'

He looked at the children again, and saw, over their clustered heads, the boat coming up on their port bow. She was some sort of cabin cruiser, not large but very stiff and serviceable. She was not hurrying, but gave the impression of power in reserve. The man at the wheel wore a beret and sun-glasses. He turned and spoke over his shoulder, and another man came out of the cabin and relieved him. The first man went below and the second, wearing a battered yachting cap and smoking a pipe, took a hand off the wheel and waved to Mr Menloe as the boats passed. Mr Menloe nodded almost imperceptibly in reply.

Paul said, 'That a Cainport boat?'

Mr Menloe nodded. 'Mr Gerard's,' he said. 'Lives over to Prytany, but he keeps her here. Goes cruising quite a bit.'

'She looks a good sea boat.'

'She's that right enough. Plenty of power there.'

'Was that Mr Gerard at the wheel?'

' 'Twas him, yes.'

'He had someone with him, I think. He only took the wheel himself as he came up to us.'

'Very likely. Didn't notice myself. There's several goes out with him.'

The blunt white bows bumped down suddenly, and a wisp of spray stood up on either side of the stem and drifted wetly down the boat. The children screamed in unison, but it was, to Paul's practised ear, a scream of pleasurable excitement purely. They wiped the salt off their eyelashes and tasted it with their tongues as it fell off the ends of their noses. They were dressed against it.

The sun came out again with a long stretch of blue sky ahead of it between the drifting clouds. The afternoon, which had been faintly sinister, suddenly held the prospect of exhilaration. Something stirred unexpectedly in the corner of Paul's left eye and he saw Mr Menloe was smiling. The effect was slightly ghastly, as if the Hound of the Baskervilles had suddenly wagged its tail. Paul tried to catch his eye, but he continued to look straight ahead. The smile died slowly. The brown skin settled into the habitual mask-lines and the moment of joviality passed without explanation.

Paul said, 'What does he call his boat, Mr Gerard?'

Mr Menloe tilted his head back. 'That one?' he said. 'Calls her *Ought-to-like-us.*' He spelt out the name *Autolycus.* 'Daft sort of name, I'd say. But 'tis wonderful the daft names people give boats.'

'Don't I know it. Has he had her long?'

'Quite a few years. She's not a new boat, of course, by any means. She's a Navy boat, we reckon, but altered a bit, and the engines is new. Mr Gerard was in the Navy, of course. He come here after the war and had her soon after. He knows what he's doing, mind, Mr Gerard. If it comes to a blow, I'd as soon be out in *Ought-to-like-us* with him as in any other boat round here.' He spat over his shoulder into the boat's wake and then, as if in obedience to some answering signal, eased her head several points westwards.

'Not that I ever have been in her,' he said. 'Nor anyone else that I know. Mr Gerard keeps her for himself and his friends he brings down with him. But he keeps her perfect, I must say.'

The sun went in again, and the boat on her new course set up a very slow corkscrew roll as she lumbered across the swell. The afternoon, which seemed determined not to commit itself, was suddenly for a second time pregnant with possible disaster.

Paul said to Mary, 'What about tea? Will they eat it? And if they will, should they? I'd like some myself, I must admit.'

'I think they will, and I'm quite sure they should.' She went forward to the bows.

She nodded to him from there, and Paul went forward with the tea basket. Tea was eaten with the desperate

149

appreciation of the winter picnic, while the boat nosed and slid her way along a savage lee shore of rocky headlands and small beaches, where the summer visitors who did not care for surf came down to bathe, but where a hard-pressed boat could find no shelter at all. Only a blunt headland, which their present course would clear easily, stood between them and the huge elliptical sweep of Bartenny Bay.

On another day and in another world only a week or so ago they had pushed out into a bay flattened like oiled silk under a weight of yellow sunlight, where the sea's movement had been undetectable except in its whispering at the foot of the cliffs. Now there was nothing but a bit of cloud and a ground swell, but the picture had changed completely. What would it have been like out here, Paul wondered, with a gale driving the whole sea forward on to the smoking cliffs and a sodden boat unhandy to windward and failing, tack after desperate tack, to make good her leeway? He shivered violently, as he remembered shivering at the inquest, and looked round guiltily, as he had then, to see whether anyone had noticed.

No one had. The sun came out suddenly upon a blue, gently rolling sea, and the bathing visitors dotted the black rocks above the beaches like pink landlocked sea-gulls. Away in the stern Mr Menloe spun the wheel and the boat put her head to sea, pitched twice in slow motion and then, with the sea now well on her quarter, turned for home.

Everything was fair about them. The fair breeze blew, the white foam, what there was of it, flew, the furrow followed free. All of them, except Mr Menloe, felt the sea in their blood, and Mr Menloe either did not feel it or had got used to the feeling. The long procession of the cliffs moved slowly back, melting and re-forming under the drifting cloud shadows. Presently Mr Menloe spat again, received, apparently, a satisfactory reply and turned the boat's head south to where the narrow cleft of Cainport was already opening to receive them.

Autolycus lay snug at her moorings. There was no one aboard and everything was shut, locked and covered in. She looked much less impressive than she had under way. They crept in under the heavy shadow of a returning cloud bank, and the children scrambled ashore as from an adventure, with no obvious reluctance. They said good-bye to Mr Menloe politely and were answered with a vestigial nod. Paul paid their hire, correctly but not generously, and they gathered themselves and moved up into the town.

Jennifer said suddenly, 'Can I have a penny? I want to be sick.'

Mary said, 'Oh Jennie, can I—?', but she shook her head, took her penny and marched resolutely off in the indicated direction.

'There's stoicism for you,' said Paul.

'It's Mr Menloe,' said Cathleen.

'Mr Menloe?'

'She couldn't be sick in front of Mr Menloe. I'd have felt the same, only I don't feel sick. Nor does Julia. It's always Jennie.'

They stood for a little in awe of this natural phenomenon, and presently Jennifer, slightly dewy but still resolute, rejoined them. The car seemed unexpectedly warm and stable. Paul, already in the driving seat, said to the car-park man, 'Whereabouts is Prytany from here?'

'Prytany? About two miles along the Clanbridge road, off to the left. But 'tis only a small place.'

Paul nodded. Mary said, 'Better not now. Ten to one his car won't be there, and we really ought to get Jennie home.'

'What did you think?'

'I thought it was him. At first it was only a mild suggestion, but then he smiled. It was after he spoke to the other man. I thought the other man spoke to him, and he simply smiled and handed over the wheel. It was very characteristic.'

'That's what I thought. And after all, why shouldn't he? But it's a splendid molehill to make a mountain out of. He's been so insistently anti-nautical, and here he is, not only on board the *Ought-to-like-us*, but apparently in full charge with the approval of the owner. And the owner gets a certificate of seaworthiness from Mr Menloe. And Mr Menloe is no enthusiast.'

'And he may or may not have recognised us before he handed over the wheel and dived below.'

'He would have, surely. He was at the wheel, and must have been watching us carefully. And there are two of us and the bunch of children, and not a pair of dark glasses between us. He couldn't have missed us. If it was him, of course.'

They came to the Pelant turning and Paul slowed down. He said to Jennifer, 'Are you all right?'

Jennifer, from the back seat, said, 'Yes.'

Cathleen, beside her, said, 'I think we ought to get home fairly soon.' Paul turned right and put his foot down.

'Yes. What the hell's that behind? Hullo!'

The long black car surged past, not roaring, but with a high continuous drone that suggested startling power. The driver half-turned as he passed, started slightly and smiled. The smile carried him past them, but almost at once the car, with a fusillade of winking and flashing lights, lost speed and began to pull in in front. Paul braked and pulled in behind it. A door opened and a pair of beautifully trousered legs swung out. A moment later Bannerman was with them, leaning on the side of the car and looking in. His smile included the whole family.

He said, 'I didn't see it was you till I was almost past. I haven't seen you around. I had begun to think you must have gone home.'

'Not till Sunday,' said Paul. Bannerman smiled and said nothing.

Mary said, 'We've been out in a boat. There was a bit of a swell, and we aren't all feeling too secure.'

'I mustn't keep you, then. If I don't see you before then, I hope you have a good journey home and will be down again next year.'

'We've just come from Cainport,' said Paul. 'We've been out with Menloe. Do you know him? All carved mahogany and general inscrutability.'

'Menloe? That will be old Menloe, I imagine, not one of his family.'

'Has he got a family? I'm surprised, I must say. I shouldn't have suspected him of the domestic tendernesses, even in his extreme youth.'

'I don't know about the tendernesses. He has – eight sons, I think it is, and most of them are married with families of their own. He's quite a patriarch, old Menloe.'

Paul laughed. 'You know everyone,' he said. 'I should have thought Cainport was off your beat a bit.'

'The Menloes have spread well beyond the limits of Cainport. I've had two of them working for me at different times. And of course the old man's well known locally. Anyway, I mustn't keep you. I may see you – next year, perhaps.' He raised a hand in salute and walked elegantly to his car. A moment later it went away in a smooth rush, like a rocket, leaving them standing.

'No change out of that,' said Paul as they moved off.

'No dogs,' said Mary. 'Don't you think he'd generally have the dogs with him if his business was on land?'

153

'It's possible. What I am really wondering is whether he would have stopped, or seen us at all, if he hadn't been looking for us.'

'But why should he look for us?'

'I think to find out, if possible, whether we had seen him or not. If that was the idea, he still doesn't know. And we still don't know for certain it was him we saw, but I don't think there can be much doubt now.'

Mary sighed. 'Do you think, in fact, it matters awfully? We shan't see him again, shall we?'

Paul said, 'I – no, I don't suppose in fact we shall.'

The car crunched on the pebbles, and they were home.

CHAPTER SEVENTEEN

'I can't serve you,' said Charles cheerfully, 'not at this time of the morning, not though you were Mr Dawson in his direst need.' He went on with his methodical washing down of the bar.

'That's all right,' said Paul. 'I didn't in fact want you to. I'm only filling in time, and thought I might as well look in. I'm going out with Mike Cardew presently.'

Charles stopped his mopping. 'Are you?' he said. 'How well do you know Mike?'

'Not well. I hardly really know him at all. I imagine you do. Tell me about him, if you will.'

Charles put down his cloth with a defiant plop. 'Tell you about him,' he said. 'Just like that. How can one ever tell anyone about anyone, except on particular terms of reference, and that's hard enough? He is tall, dark and so beautiful the sense faints picturing him. But you probably know that, or at least your wife will have pointed it out.

Less obviously, he is intelligent. He is what they used to call superior, and probably still do down here. That means that he is so much better than his parents that he might even in time be nearly as good as you are – never quite, of course. He won't stoop to talking nice, though no doubt he could if he tried. Finally, he is a friend of mine.'

'Lor, lor,' said Paul, 'how you jump down my throat. There is really no need to get up on such a very high and mettlesome horse. I only asked you to tell me about him. And how very well, if you did but know it, you do. And about yourself, of course.'

Charles grinned. It was his indefeasible good temper, Paul thought, that saved him time and again from the worst excesses of coltishness. 'All right, all right,' he said. 'I'm sorry. I'm afraid I was guilty of crying before Mike was hurt. The instinct wasn't essentially ignoble, do you think?' He looked at Paul anxiously.

'Not ignoble at all. And only a little bit silly. Undiscriminating rather than indiscreet. You saw me, as it were, drive up to Mike's door and rushed out shooting wildly in all directions, regardless of the fact that I had only come to read the gas meter.'

'Well. All right. I can't help wondering about that gas meter, all the same. You've been out in Mike's boat once with the whole family. I admit that doesn't make for close personal contact, and of course Mike isn't all that forthcoming. On this occasion, if it is not indiscreet to ask, are you travelling *en masse* or *in loco parentis*?'

'*In loco*—? Oh, I see. I suppose that's why you were so fierce and indignant on his behalf. That in itself seems significant.'

Charles said, 'Before you go nap on its significance, may I say that I haven't myself talked to Mike about all this. I know the facts, because I seem to know nearly everything that happens. But I can't, even if I wanted to, give you an inside picture, except in so far as I know Mike a good deal better than you do, and can therefore make a more intelligent guess. And if you're going to talk to him, your guess will be, to say the least, as good as mine. But at this stage, for what it's worth, it's Mike I'm worried about, not the girl.'

'Do you remember Mr Bannerman on that subject? That morning in here after we had been talking to Mr Dawson. He was afraid some girl would get her hooks into him and give him ambitions ashore. Is that your worry?'

Charles considered this. 'In a way, perhaps,' he said. 'It's more that I don't want him hurt. He could be very vulnerable, particularly to attack from a certain quarter.'

'I wish you'd explain that. What sort of quarter?'

Charles smiled. 'Damn you,' he said, 'you're going to make me sound silly or worse. But I may as well say what I mean. I think a woman with more education and confidence and – oh hell, polish generally than he's used to might make real trouble for him.'

Paul said, 'What you are trying to say is that Mike might get hurt by falling in love out of his own class. But you jib at the word because you think the thing itself is wrong. I can't think why. There is a real difficulty here. I have already considered it, as a matter of fact, though from the the other side of the fence, so to speak. Doesn't it occur to you that, whatever other factors there are, this girl is very young and – simple, in a way?'

'I don't know her, you see, any more than you know Mike. I know she's very young and very quiet, and doesn't give much away, because she is in a state of more or less permanent reaction to her dreadful parents. You say she's simple. All right, that's fine. I still see her as a possible disruptive influence. I've told you, I haven't discussed it and I don't know what Mike's attitude is. But if he were at any point inclined to take her seriously, I should be pretty thoroughly worried.'

'It hasn't occurred to you that the boot might be on the the other foot? Apart from anything else, there's Mike's looks. Any woman might fall heavily for him, and if she was young and simple, it mightn't be him that suffered.'

'She'd get over it, I expect. I can't see her in any other sort of trouble. Mike's a serious sort of chap, and I can't see him – what's the phrase? – taking advantage of a young girl's affection. If he wasn't interested in her, she wouldn't get much change out of him. She'd just have to get over it as best she could.'

'Lord,' said Paul, 'you don't make much pretence at impartiality, do you? It's Mike that must be protected. The girl can look after herself.'

Charles looked at him blankly. 'That's as I see it,' he said. 'He's worth six of her.'

'Stuff and pompous male nonsense,' said Paul. 'You admit you don't know her. How dare you write her down like that just because you're a friend of Mike's?'

Charles smiled suddenly. 'I tell you one thing,' he said. 'I'm damn glad to hear her so hotly championed. I admit I don't know her. But your attitude makes me think there must be more to her than meets the eye.'

'That's bloody handsome of you,' said Paul. He was still angry, but knew from experience that it was very difficult to be angry with Charles for long. 'Anyway, I must go and meet this sensitive plant of yours. Perhaps then I shall be able to form a balanced judgment.'

The wind of yesterday had gone, and the hurrying cloudbank had drifted to a halt. The river lay like a steel sheet under a damp, translucent air. Even with the season nearly over the most sanguine dinghy sailor could not put himself to the trouble of running a sail up. The tide moved silently between the dark green shores and nothing moved on it at all.

Paul heard the thud of Cardew's engine long before he saw the boat, and when the boat came in sight, it looked very small in the grey void. Cardew stood upright, head back, one hand on the wheel, in sole but unconscious possession of a vast stage. He seemed not so much to concentrate on the handling of the boat as to use it unconsciously, as if it was part of himself, as the means of his own movement through the grey silence. He cut the engine and drifted down to where Paul was standing. Both men, as though at a word of command, lifted their hands in salute and dropped them again. The boat nosed in and Paul clambered aboard. Then she backed off, turned and started down-river. Paul sat in the stern sheets and could see, even from behind him, that Cardew looked a little tense. The whole thing ought to be embarrassing, but he was not conscious of any embarrassment. All he felt was a reluctance to break the peace of the morning by talking at all. He would have been happy to drift on indefinitely through this grey and liquid world. He remembered Susan saying, 'We never talk about anything on shore at all once we're away. It's as though it didn't exist.'

He roused himself. It was Susan he had come to talk about. He said, 'It's nice of you to let me come. I wanted to talk to you.'

'Yes?' said Cardew 'Well, I didn't think you'd come just for the trip.' He sounded equable but noncommittal.

Paul said, 'You may think it's no business of mine. Nor is it, if you like to look at it in that way. I have no rights in the matter and no responsibilities. I wanted to talk to you because I'm worried, and I'd like to get things a bit clearer in my own mind, whether or not I can do anything about them. But I've no more footing than that.'

'No? Well, that's fair enough. What is it you're worried about, then?'

'I'm worried about Susan Frayne.'

There was no mistaking the surprise. Cardew swung half round, and the boat, which was so much part of the man, swung first one way and then the other as he jerked her off course and righted her again instinctively. He gave Paul a quick, questioning look and turned back to his steering. He said, 'Susan Frayne? Why should you be worried about her?' The tone was unexpected. There was a hint of anger in it, but a kind of lightness, as though a mounting tension had been suddenly relieved.

Paul, disconcerted, hesitated and picked his words with care. 'She's been coming out with you pretty well daily this last week or so. She hasn't told her parents or, up to the day before yesterday, anyone else where she has been. She's been making you pick her up down-river, where no one was supposed to see. Now, of course, people have seen her out with you and are starting to talk. It's her making such a mystery of it that's half the trouble. You can understand that.'

'How do you know all this?'

'Susan told us. She's – well, a bit unhappy and confused in her mind, and I asked her whether she would mind my talking to you about it. She agreed – a bit doubtfully, I admit. Anyway, she knows I am going to talk to you.'

'I'm sorry. I still don't rightly know what you're worried about.'

'Several things. The secrecy, to begin with.'

'That wasn't my doing.'

'I know that. But you aren't going to tell me you didn't know about it.'

'No. All right. I did know pretty well she was coming

159

out on the sly, but I can't say I saw much harm in it. I haven't thought about it much, to tell you the truth. I imagine she reckoned her parents wouldn't think me proper company for their daughter and wasn't going to tell them for fear they'd put a stop to it. Well. I don't know your views, but so far as I'm concerned, to hell with all that. The girl was bored to death ashore and happy afloat. And I liked having her company. And she wasn't misbehaving herself – not with me, anyway. So I reckoned if her parents would object, she had a right not to tell them.'

'I'm with you all the way up to the last bit. Making a secret of a thing's always liable to cause trouble. Also – and this is really where we come into it – her parents think she's been spending the time with us. We haven't told them she hasn't. But we can't go on letting them think that now we know about it. I feel fully justified in not making trouble over what's happened, but I can't play gooseberry deliberately.'

'What do you want me to do then? Refuse to take her, or go and ask the colonel's consent to me squiring his daughter?'

'I tell you, to be honest, I don't know what's the best thing to do. I think it depends a lot on your attitude.'

'My attitude to what?'

'To Susan mainly. You say you like having her company. You know she's happy with you. But things having started the way they have, it's liable to cause trouble if it goes on. The question is, is it worth it?'

Cardew did not answer. The boat crept under the dark cone of Skittle Hill and out into an expanse of breathless, steel-grey sea. A gull, motionless on the motionless water, seemed so bemused by the quiet that it could hardly stir itself from the boat's path. A last-minute flick of the wheel avoided it and left it bobbing, indignant but still bemused, on the oily ripples of the wake.

Cardew said, 'Don't it make you sick, when you come to think of it? What's wrong with us, anyway? There's nothing to be ashamed of, is there, if Susan likes coming out and I like taking her? She's good in a boat, you know. She doesn't know much yet, but it comes naturally to her. If her father would take his daughter in that dinghy of his instead of someone else's daughter all the time, he'd know that. But that's not the point. She likes coming with me and I like having her. And if all the old cats in the parish liked to come along too, they'd not see anything they could make a fuss about. It's nothing but bloody snobbery – that with some and just dirty minds with others.'

'I know all that,' said Paul. 'I've been over all this with Susan. But it doesn't really answer my question. Contemptible or not, the objections are there; and Susan has preferred to come out, as you say, on the sly rather than face up to them. That can't go on. The question is whether it is worth it to you to defy the objections or whether it is better to give it up. And as I say, that seems to me to depend on your attitude to Susan. She's the one that's going to suffer, whatever happens. You know that, unless you're a lot more of a fool than I take you for. You're sitting pretty by comparison. She's either got to face a lot of unpleasantness and seriously upset her father – and for all his faults she's still quite fond of him – or stop coming out with you. And that would damn near break her heart. You know she's in love with you, don't you?'

Cardew said nothing for some time. Then he said, 'She's very young still.'

'She'll be eighteen next month. That's not too young to be pretty seriously in love.'

'I didn't want her to be in love with me.'

'You mean you didn't make love to her. I know that.

But don't tell me you didn't know. You must have had women falling in love with you at pretty regular intervals for years now. You can't tell me you don't know it when you see it.'

'All right. I did know. I knew she was in love with me, and I liked it. But I hadn't intended it or encouraged it. You think I took advantage of her being lonely and bored. I tell you, when she first started coming out with me, I was as lonely as she was and a bloody sight more miserable. I still am, if it comes to that, and there's not much anybody can do about it. But Susan helped, just being there. She's a good girl, you know.'

'I know how good she is. I've no doubt she was a help to you. But didn't it occur to you that she was helping to patch up your broken heart, if that was what you were suffering from, only at the risk of breaking her own? I admit you played fair by her in a way. You haven't given her any ground for thinking you're interested in her. But have you ever told her you're not? It's all very well being companionable and decent and noncommittal and I expect a bit pathetic, but that's not going to stop her falling in love with you. For the matter of that, it might have been better if you had made up to her a bit. She'd soon have seen it wasn't serious and that might have put her on her guard. I don't mean against you – I mean against herself, her own feelings. As it was, the thing could go on indefinitely, with Susan getting deeper in all the time, but never giving up hope. God knows I'm not here to lecture you, but I do want you to see what her position is. What you do about it is your own affair. I don't doubt you'll do what you can.'

For the second time Cardew did not reply. The boat moved on steadily over the limitless grey and Paul noticed, as he had noticed before, how the pulse of the engine and the wash of the boat seemed to intensify the silence rather than break it.

Finally Cardew turned and looked at him, and the indignation he had been working up on Susan's behalf was melted by the unmistakable unhappiness of the dark, expressive face.

Cardew said, 'How old are you?'

'A dozen years older than you, at least.'

'I wondered. You talked about broken hearts. I wondered – I'm not trying to be rude, mind – but I wondered if you knew what you were talking about?'

'At your age? Oh yes, I know what I'm talking about. But it's got to be an older woman, not a girl like Susan.'

'That's right. Well. You knew Mrs Trent, didn't you?'

'Mrs Trent? I knew her, yes. I didn't know you did.'

'Oh yes.' He laughed, so that Paul could hardly bear to hear him. 'To tell the truth, I thought it was that you wanted to talk about. She was coming to meet me when it happened. And I still don't know how it happened, nor where. I tell you, it's damned near driving me crazy.'

CHAPTER EIGHTEEN

'You?' said Paul. 'Of course, why not? I just never thought. I'm sorry. You never saw her that day at all?'

Cardew shook his head, and for a long time there was silence. Then he said, 'You'll see now why I – why things stand as they do with Susan. I didn't want you to think— She's a good kid. I'm fond of her, if you like, and I needed someone. But I hadn't got anything left to give her. I couldn't – well, blast it, what I said. She's just a nice kid. Mrs Trent was all any man ever dreamt of.'

163

Paul said nothing. He watched the immobile back and thought how unlike Cardew was to the Bywaters he and the sergeant had invented.

Presently Cardew spoke again, almost as if he spoke to the empty sea ahead. 'I don't suppose you'd understand,' he said. 'You might. I don't know. I've never had much to do with women. The older ones frighten me and the girls make me sick. The ones I know, anyway. I know I attract them, but it doesn't seem to add up. Mrs Trent – it sounds daft, but I'd rather call her that, do you mind? – she made everything – well, straightforward. It's difficult to explain. Like in a dream, do you know? Nothing seemed to need saying. I was down with the boat one evening, late, and she came down, walking quite slowly over the beach, but walking straight to me. She was – well, you knew her. There was something in her, physically, that just melted your bones. She said, "Will you come with me?" That's all. I left the boat and we walked into the dunes. I'd never made love before, in fact. That'd surprise you, I expect, with your picture of the working class. You'd probably think I'd been putting fat fisher girls over lobster pots since I was sixteen. Not that it made any difference. Whatever I'd done, I'd have learnt it all over again with Mrs Trent. Nothing I'd ever known would have made sense after her. But in fact she was the first, whether she knew it or not. I expect she did. We did talk, of course – about everything under the sun after we'd finished with ourselves. She was a wonderful talker, you know. Well – listener, perhaps. I expect I did most of the talking. But she knew what I was talking about, and I talked differently because of it. Like a different language, do you see? I've always been afraid of talking educated. Except lately, of course, with Susan. I could talk to Mrs Trent and not worry.'

164

Paul suddenly saw he was smiling. 'Not like *Lady Chatterley's Lover* at all. That was a daft book, if ever. Do you remember? Chap couldn't make love except in working class language. I don't know. Mrs Trent's being a lady was very important to me. But feeling like that didn't make me feel a snob. You didn't have to pretend anything with her at all. I just didn't think about it.'

Paul said, 'I've heard someone else say that,' but he did not think Cardew heard him. He waited a minute and then said, 'How long was this before she was drowned?'

'A week. No more. We met five times, but it was difficult. There are always people everywhere in the summer. She was on at me to find somewhere we could have completely to ourselves. But it had to be near. We hadn't got cars. I had the boat, of course, but I couldn't take her in it without someone seeing. In the end I said the Glyn. I didn't mean to, really, but she jumped at it. We were going to meet there that day, but she never came. I never saw her at all. I never saw her again, do you see? I'll get over it, of course. But nothing'll ever be the same now. I don't rightly know what to do with myself sometimes.'

He broke off again. Paul said, 'This place you were going to meet. You called it the Glyn. I've never heard of it.'

Cardew looked round at him suddenly and then away again. 'Did I say that?' he said. 'I didn't mean to. Not that it matters anyway. Only I wish I'd never told her. That's right, the Glyn. You'll never have heard of it, of course. Nor has anyone else that I know of. My dad showed it to me. He said he didn't think anyone else remembered it, and I've told no one. It's a cave, sort of.'

'Out on Bartenny?'

'That's right.'

'Look, I don't want to worry you, but I do very much

165

wish you'd tell me a bit more about it. You say she never got there. How was she getting there? On foot, I imagine?'

'She was going along the cliff. I was going later by sea. She should have been there first and waited for me. When I got there, she wasn't there. I knew she'd started much earlier. I knew she couldn't just be late. I had to go at once or much later. I decided to go and see if I could find her. But I never did.'

'How were you getting there then? You can't land any-where from the sea on Bartenny and you can't get down to the sea from the top of the cliff. At least, that's what I've been told.'

'So you would too. Only it's wrong, because there is the Glyn. But as I say no one knows about it. It was known once, of course. They used it a lot for smuggling. But that went out and it's been forgotten. Only my dad knew, and he showed me, as I told you.'

'I don't see – it doesn't really seem possible. Mr Banner-man doesn't know about it, and he lives on Bartenny. He told me there was no way down to the sea and nowhere you could beach a boat except one cove on the eastern side.'

'That'd be Maiden Cove. That's right, you can put a boat in there anywhere under half-tide, but you can't get up the cliff from there, nor down to it. But Mr Bannerman wouldn't know about the Glyn. He's not been here more than fifteen years, and he came from up country. And any-way you don't beach a boat in the Glyn – you run clean in. I haven't done it but two or three times, to make sure I could, since my dad showed me. It's a tricky business even under power. How they did it under sail I don't know, but they must have, away back. Or they rowed in, perhaps. That'd be it, because of the height as you go in.'

'Where is it, then? Why can't you see it from the sea?'

'You can, but it doesn't look anything special. It's right opposite the Tabernacles. You take your bearing from them, so far as you can without a second mark out to sea. And you get your tide level from them. That's the important thing. There's only a matter of feet in it. It comes about half-ebb.'

'That's when you get the big tide-run through between the Tabernacles and the head.'

'That's right. That's the difficulty. You can't do it at all except in the right conditions. Then you come in slow with the current, from east to west, turn her head in and then shoot the mouth as the tide takes your stern round. You've got to be well fendered even so. She generally scrapes a bit. You're all right for water so long as you come in at just the right state of the tide. As I say, you get that best from the Tabernacles. It doesn't last twenty minutes. If it's too high there's no headroom and if it's too low you'll take the rock going in and maybe rip the bottom out of her. I told you it was tricky.'

'But when you're in, then what? You say you can't beach her. What do you do?'

'Float. There's a deep-water pool that never empties. Like a natural dock. There's a bit of a beach above, but you couldn't put a boat on it. She floats there till the half-flood. Then you take her out quick at the right moment. If you missed it, you'd be caught. The cave fills pretty well right up. You could get up the cliff, of course, if you knew the way, but the boat would be swamped and sunk. But like that, once you're in, you've got between half-ebb and half-flood. No one can get in, not from the sea, that is. They could come down from the top if they knew the way. But no one does that I know of.'

'Have you ever been in the cave that long?'

'Me? No. I told you, I've only been in two or three

times, and I always came straight out. I didn't like the idea of getting caught.'

'You haven't explored the cave itself much?'

'Not explored it, no. But there's nothing really. Just the basin, as I said, and a bit of beach above it.'

'This way up – where does it come out? I've been all round the head, and there's nothing like a path going down.'

'There wouldn't be. To tell you the truth, I've never been down from the top. I've been up from the bottom nearly to the top, but I never went right up for fear of being seen if there was anyone about on the head. But I know where it comes out, of course. There again – it doesn't look anything from the top. You've got to know it's there or you'd never believe it. There's a steep slope below the coastguard's path to what looks like the edge of the cliff. There's gorse at the bottom of the slope. You go through the gorse and round a rock. The path's there all right. A bit frightening if you don't like heights, but safe enough. Further down it comes right out round a shoulder of the cliff. You can even see that bit from the top at one place. All these years since my dad died I've been the only person that knew about the Glyn. And then I told Mrs Trent. We'd have been there, you see, from half-ebb to half-flood that day. Only she never came.'

'Do you mind telling me your plan? I'm sorry, but it's important.'

'Well. I told you, more or less. Mrs Trent was going to walk out to the head at lunch time. The tide was already falling then, but it wouldn't be till quite a bit later I'd be able to get the boat into the Glyn. Only we thought that if she went then, no one would suspect anything and there'd be less likely anyone about on the head. I told her where the path came down. She couldn't have missed it if she got that far. She was going to go down as far as she could, where she'd be out of anyone's sight, and wait for me to bring the boat in at half-ebb. I went out some time after her. I went through between the Tabernacles and the head. I couldn't see anyone anywhere. Well, I couldn't have seen Mrs Trent anyway, you see, if she'd been where she should have been. Then when the tide was right I came in, as I told you, along with the tide run and put her into the Glyn. I got her in all right, but Mrs Trent wasn't there. I left the boat floating and went up almost to the top of he path, but there was no sign of her. Then I had to decide quick, you see. I could wait for the half-flood, as we'd planned, in the hope that she'd come, or I could get out quick and go and look for her. It didn't seem any good waiting. She should have been there long before me. Anyway, I decided to get out. I ran down and got the boat out on just about the last of the water, and even then I scraped her a bit. I worked back along under Bartenny looking for her. You can see the coastguard path nearly all the way back to the east end of Lanting, you know – well, you've been out there, you know. If she'd been anywhere on the path I'd have seen her. But there was no one. I didn't know what had happened, but I reckoned she must have been stopped somehow on the way out. I heard a rumour that night that she was missing, but I didn't know what I could do. Then next day I heard she'd been found.'

'The police did get on to you, didn't they?'

'That's right. I told them I'd been out there. Not about the Glyn, of course, nor what I'd gone there for. I told them I hadn't seen Mrs Trent, which was true. I didn't see, and I still don't, what call there was to tell them anything more. So I said nothing. Then when you wanted to come out today, I thought you were going to ask me about it. I knew you were interested, and I thought perhaps someone might have seen something I didn't know of. I was surprised when it turned out to be Susan. I hadn't given her much of a thought, poor kid. I'm sorry that had to happen. As I said, I'm fond of her, and I didn't want to make her unhappy. But I wasn't really in a mood to worry much and that's the truth.'

'You haven't told her about you and Mrs Trent?'

'I haven't told anyone, not till now.'

Paul thought. 'Susan was fond of her, you know,' he said. 'And although you say she's young, she's very well aware of things. I mean, she wouldn't be shocked or horrified. It's one of those things only you can judge, but I'm inclined to think it wouldn't be a bad thing if you told her, if you can bring yourself to it. I think it might help you both. And look,' he said after a pause, 'whatever you do, don't cease to be grateful for Mrs Trent. She'll never, as it is, mean anything but warmth and sweetness to you, and some of the sweetness will stay with you if you live to be a hundred. It mightn't have been so, you know, if she had lived. That's not just routine cynicism. The danger is always there. It might have been all right. But you may be luckier than some of us. I don't want to be impertinent, but I think you should try to convince yourself of that.'

Cardew nodded. He said, 'What are you going to do now? About Mrs Trent, I mean. Do you think you know what happened?'

'Not yet. There are a few pointers perhaps.'

'You won't – I don't want it known about her and me. I couldn't stand for that.'

'I know. So far as I can I promise that. But I'm very glad you told me. And I'll want to go and have a look at that cave of yours.'

Cardew shrugged. 'I don't mind that,' he said. 'Not

now.' He went about his business silently in the profound grey silence, and all the while the world darkened round them. It was as they turned finally for home that he put his head up and seemed to be listening or even, like a dog, sampling the almost motionless air in his nostrils. "Tis going to blow,' he said.

'When and how much?'

'By this evening it will be up, I reckon. Not that hard, but enough to put the sea up a bit. You'll see all the dinghies come running out when it first blows up, and there'll be some of them turn over before they're safe home again. But they seem to like it, so why worry? It's what they come for, after all.'

They were back in the river again when Cardew said, 'I've been thinking. What I told you about the way it started. Must have sounded a bit shameless. The lady of experience seducing her innocent inferior. More like Potiphar's wife than Lady Chatterley. But it wasn't like that.'

Paul said nothing. Cardew said, 'It's so hard not to give you a wrong picture of her. It's like a dream. I said that before. But I don't mean because it was sudden and didn't last. That's not it. It was like a dream at the time, do you see? My dream, that's the point. It's as if she had come out of my own mind and was part of myself. There's no shame between one part of your mind and another. I'm not much good at explaining.'

'On the contrary,' said Paul, 'you explain it almost better than I can bear.'

'Not that it matters I suppose, what you think. Only now I've told you, for some reason I don't want you to get it wrong. If it makes you feel a bit sick, I haven't explained it at all.'

Paul said, 'It makes me feel nothing but very old and

very sad. Most men are alike, you know, except the hearties who put fat fisher girls over lobster pots. Only we don't all have our dreams come walking to us across the beach on a late summer evening. You've just been lucky, that's all. I suppose some day you'll see it.'

He left the boat at the water's edge and walked up under a lowering sky. A long finger of cold air stroked his left cheek, and he turned to find the whole river burnished with the black and silver fish scales of the awakening wind. An eager, boyish man in a yellow life-jacket said, 'It's coming up, thank God. We'll get a sail this evening yet.' The yacht club hard was a scene of excited activity. Full of a nameless and bottomless depression, Paul picked his way through it and made for his car. The wind, freshening all the time, followed him home to Lanting.

CHAPTER NINETEEN

Paul looked at the notice and hesitated. THERE IS NO WAY DOWN TO THE SEA. THESE CLIFFS ARE DANGEROUS. The wind tugged at his clothes and below him the whole sea moved eastwards, line upon line, towards the foot of the black, invisible cliffs. Millie had come this way on a golden and placid afternoon. If she had read the notice, she had probably laughed at it, having other things in mind. A sea-cave idyll, thought Paul, reverting to a previous line of thought. An idyll in the purest classical tradition. The goddess and the beautiful young fisherman. Only somewhere between the stone stile and her expected idyll someone or something had caught up with her. He climbed the stile and went steadily along the path.

The fence fell away on his right, and as he started his

climb towards the head, the sun came out suddenly, turning the whole expanse of moving sea a pale and windy
gold. As Cardew had said, it was not a gale, but it blew
steadily from the west, and the rolling masses of water that
marched on Bartenny had come a long way. At any time
now the tide would start to run westwards between
Bartenny and the Tabernacles, straight into the teeth of
the sea. Murder, Cardew had said. Murder, at any rate,
murder of one sort or another there did seem to have been,
not very far from here and not very long ago. He leant
sideways against the wind and went on climbing.

The path flattened suddenly and swung right. There
were the Tabernacles below him, no longer lying on a
level sea, but crouched defiantly, taking the sea in a welter
of spray and churned water on their battered western end.
To his right, and visible through a green funnel of cliff, a
spur of rock ran sheer down to the water. He saw a faint
line drawn diagonally across it not far above water level,
and wondered whether this was the place Cardew had
mentioned, where the path down to the Glyn was
momentarily visible from the cliff top. From where he was
it looked uninviting.

The path turned again, and here was the steep green
slope and the gorse clinging to its lower end, almost at the
cliff's edge. Here, if Cardew was to be believed, there was
despite all appearances a path through the gorse, round
the grey spike of rock that showed above it and down the
cliff face to the forgotten cave at its foot. He had no doubt
Cardew was to be believed. The path was undoubtedly
there. He still did not want to go down it.

He turned sideways to the slope and, left foot leading,
edged down towards the gorse bushes. There was in fact
an opening between the roots, though the bushes had grown
together over it. He put a foot in and found the way, at

173

ground level, clear ahead. From the waist down he forced himself between the converging bushes, following the line found for him by his invisible feet. The path was there all right.

Suddenly the bushes thinned in front of him and he found the sea, angry and incredibly remote, almost vertically beneath him. His feet led to the right, and his hands reached and fastened on the lichened spike of overhanging rock. Round its base, and then doubling back under the fold of the cliff, a narrow but perfectly negotiable path led sharply downwards. He set his feet, now clear of the gorse, on the granite gravel of the path and leant back against the rock. He considered his solid corduroys and remembered Millie's clinging sharkskin. He wondered whether she had got this far. The doctor hadn't mentioned scratches on her legs, but surely the gorse would have marked her if she had forced her way through as he had done. Perhaps not. For all the riches of her physique, her legs had been slender and the pressure would have been much less. Come to that, he doubted whether his own skin was marked, even where the prickles had got through. Gorse was not blackthorn. No, there was no reason to think Millie had not got this far. And it was presumably about to this point that Cardew, desperate for time with the tide running out under his boat in the cave below, had climbed the path looking for her and had not found her. He seemed no nearer his answer, but must at least carry his exploration through.

He got his weight cautiously on to his feet. The wind pushed intermittently at his back, and below him a long rolling sea suddenly reared up and threw off its top in a flurry of white water as the tide-rip undercut its base. Out of sight of everything but the sea, and unrecognisable even from there, the path worked its way dizzily but solidly round and always down the black, overhanging rock face.

He did not attempt to reckon, from here, where exactly it was leading him. In front of him now, and still a long way below him, he saw the black spur he had seen for a moment from the top of the cliff, with the path, clearly visible now, threading its way diagonally across it. The Glyn must be just on the far side of the spur. From down here the Tabernacles presented a much broader flank to the headland, and the cave mouth could be anywhere in thirty or forty yards of cliff and still be, near enough, opposite them.

His skin and clothes were sticky now with the salt dampness of the buffeting air. The tumult of the sea, thrown up by the upsurge of air and bandied about in the crags and hollows of the cliff, seemed to deaden his other senses. Cautiously, with half-closed eyes and tentative feet, he worked his way down the path towards the white ferment below. He went very slowly. The tide was barely yet at half-ebb, and although he was coming to it from above, he wanted to see the cave as it would be when a boat could get into it. There was plenty of time. His stomach was full of a sick apprehension, but reason told him he was safe enough. As Cardew had said, the path, given ordinary caution, was not dangerous.

The path dipped sharply and turned left. He was getting near the root of the spur. He stopped, steadied himself against the rock face on his right and looked down. The sea was hardly more than thirty feet below him now, though the rise and fall of the water, as the seas poured themselves along the broken rocks, in itself accounted for six or eight feet. Once more he transferred his weight to his feet and went on down the path. This was the spur now.

The path here, for the first time, was unmistakably unsafe, at least in present conditions. It had a shelving rock

175

surface, sticky with salt and sharply undercut. Above it, the rock leant well back, and providing he used his feet cautiously, there should be no difficulty in keeping his balance. Without pausing to consider the matter too carefully, he spread his hands on the rock and edged out along the face of the spur. The gusts here flattened him against the wall, and the sea sucked and roared at the rock not very far below. He turned his face to the cliff and, placing his feet with exaggerated deliberation, went spreadeagled and crabwise down the path.

The bullet hit the rock six inches clear of his right hand, scattering him with splintered granite. For all the roar of the sea, the sound of the shot was deafeningly loud. He let go his right hand, swung half-round and felt one foot slip on the edge of the path. That second shot struck a foot to the left and level with his face. He flinched away from it, slipped and came down on his knees on the path, clawing with his hands at the unresponsive rock face above him. Then his knees went over the edge and he hung, first by his elbows and then by his hands, from the edge of the path. His feet reached desperately for a hold below him, but the rock was too much undercut. He tried to pull himself back, but knew at once that his fingers could not long maintain their present hold, much less serve to pull him back. He kicked sideways, and as he swung with his kicking leg, his left hand lost its grip. For a moment he hung by his right hand, his mind a blank, his face staring into a white buckskin shoe wedged solidly into a crevice of the black rock. Then he started to fall.

He was not conscious of hitting the water, but felt it close over him and roar in his ears as the fall carried him under. Short of breath from his struggle on the path, he kicked desperately to bring himself to the top and felt one foot strike glancingly against a submerged rock. He broke

176

surface, gulped a lungful of air and with the instinct born of experience struck out wildly for open water. The sea was on him at once, rolling over him and dashing itself in his face, so that for all his need it seemed impossible to fill his lungs with air without risking that fatal instantaneous inhalation of salt water that has sunk so many strong swimmers in a breaking sea. Clear of the immediate danger of the rocks, he lay limp, pitching heavily in the steep seas like a waterlogged boat, as he pulled first one arm and then the other out of his jacket sleeves and let the encumbrance slide away into deep water. He lifted his head to take stock of his position, and saw with a momentary sick anxiety that the tide had already sucked him clear of the cliff and was sweeping him steadily out into the middle of the channel. Swimming as he could, but concentrating all the forces of his mind on the business of breathing and keeping afloat, he seemed incapable of making any decision what he should try to do.

His drift was now clearly outwards, across the channel. The wind on the one hand and the tide on the other struggled for the limp possession of him, so that he moved neither eastwards with the one nor westwards with the other, but always northwards, to where the white waters boiled with their irreconcilable fury.

A wave broke on top of him, driving him down and rolling tumultuously over him, so that he thought he would never be free of it. When he got his head out and, regardless of the risk involved, gulped a long breath of air, he suddenly knew what he had to do. His only hope was the Tabernacles. He was still mainly east of them, and if he could make this, their lee side, there was a chance of getting out of the sea alive. Once through the channel to westwards he saw no hope of making land anywhere before he went under from exhaustion. Head down, with a calm

177

desperation of settled purpose, he swam heavily north-wards through the outrageous sea.

The distance was not great, but he knew it was the ut-most limit of his powers. Gradually, nursing his strength as best he could and always with three-quarters of his mind bent on the basic struggle for clear air to breathe, he edged nearer to the long slopes of rock. Then, as the power of the wind lessened, the tide took hold of him in good earn-est, and he saw that he was already losing his battle for the lee side. Fighting his way forward desperately in a calmer but now more dangerous sea, he saw the long black rock slide slowly across his path. He lashed out in a sort of frenzy and took a wave full in his open mouth. For a moment everything stopped working. Head back, arms threshing idly, his body hung between life and death and his mind teetered perilously on the verge of unconscious-ness. Then from some unknown reserve of nervous energy his diaphragm kicked up the last remnants of used air out of tortured lungs to blow the channels clear and, utterly at the mercy of the sea but once more back in the fight, he drew in a long breath of air, coughed violently, inhaled again and knew that for a strictly limited time he was yet capable of saving himself.

He swam forward half-a-dozen strokes, felt the sea take hold of him again and then, before he was ready for it, was face to face with the final danger. He was close to the rocks now, but almost under their weather face, where the sea broke tumultuously on a series of receding ledges. So far from not making the rocks, he could not now avoid them. The question was whether he could survive the impact and get ashore unbroken.

As he watched, the sea drew back from the huge face of rock, uncovering as it fell ledge below ledge, while the water left behind poured down in seething cascades over the glistening edges, and he felt himself sucked back and down almost to the floor of the sea. Then a great surge of sea rose under him, lifted him helplessly higher and higher in a flurry of breaking water and then, without pause or respite, hurled him bodily at the black face of the rock.

His feet, mercifully still strongly shod, struck twice sharply as the rock rose under him. Then with his left elbow and the right side of his chest he came full on to a convex slope of ridged rock. For all the suddenness of the shock, the solidity steadied him. This, despite its menace, was salvation, and he must not let it go. Head down, hands torn and bleeding, every muscle strained in his last extremity, he hung on while the great surge of water swept over him, trying to tear him upwards from his hold and then, almost without pause or warning, fell back and tried to beat him down into the depths from which he had come. Instantaneously, and with perfect clarity, there came into his mind the picture of Odysseus, clinging to the rocky edge of Phaeacia with both hands, while the great sea rolled over him. Odysseus had been sucked back, torn from his rock like a cuttlefish. The word κοτυληδονόφιν danced in his mind. Suckers, it meant. It was an archaic case-ending that had re-emerged delightfully from the Linear-B tablets, or so he seemed to remember.

He roused himself. He was crouched on a sloping rock face, hardly more than semi-conscious, but momentarily clear of the water. Sobbing, audibly but unconsciously, as Odysseus had sobbed, he began to scramble up the rocks, noticing with a kind of mild bewilderment that all his limbs seemed to be working normally. More by instinct than by observation he sensed the fresh onset of the sea behind him. He flung himself again on his face, feet and hands dug well into the rounded ribs of the rock, and for the last time the sea rolled over him, bellowing and tugging

179

him first one way and then the other. But here its strength was less. Face down in the cascading salt, Paul grinned savagely. He had beaten it. It wouldn't get him now. The air round his head cleared, and he began to crawl upwards again.

Away across the flurry of breaking seas he saw out of the corner of his eye the black land mass of Bartenny tower above him, and noticed with a kind of indignation that the sea breaking at its foot did not from here look particularly large or menacing. He stopped on a ledge and watched confusedly while a long arm of seething water reached out from below and washed round his ankles. Gradually out of the turmoil of his mind one fact emerged and nagged at him for attention. Someone up on Bartenny had shot at him. Whether or not they had shot to kill, they had shot him down into the sea with only a poor chance of getting out of it alive. He shivered violently, and a fresh wave of hopelessness closed over him. Whoever they were, they could still be up there, watching him. And it was from Bartenny, if anywhere, that his rescue must come.

He struggled a few more feet up the rock, where not even the biggest sea could reach him, and leant his head on his arms. He shivered fiercely and spasmodically, and noticed for the first time that his left arm and both knees streamed steadily with blood under his sodden clothes. The noise of the sea, which had seemed to lessen as he crawled clear of the water, re-asserted itself in his consciousness. It made him horribly afraid. He put his hands over his ears like a frightened child and leant back against the rock. Give me time to recover myself, he thought. I'll think of something. But he did not know what it could be.

Something white showed for a moment round the black

shoulder of rock and disappeared again. He put his hands down and stared incredulously. Then he opened his mouth and tried to shout, but no sound came. Butting her way doggedly into the steep seas, not more than fifteen yards out in the channel, a white boat, hidden intermittently in a flurry of breaking water, came slowly into his field of vision.

This time he shouted, though it did not seem possible he could be heard. He stumbled down the rock, waving his hands convulsively. Then a dark form in the bows of the pitching boat waved in reply and he knew he had been seen. Something melted inside him, and he began to cry, softly but with an unspeakable happiness.

The boat was still some way east of where he stood, making way cautiously into the breaking sea. The figure beckoned to him. He stopped crying and his heart turned over. He knew what he had to do, and his whole physical nature clamoured to him not to do it. But the boat could not get to him, nor, having once gone past, could she turn in that sea and come back. She could only go steadily past where he stood. The rest he must do for himself.

Susan, standing erect in the bucking bows, beckoned him again with a touch of desperation, and he saw that she held a coiled line. Blindly and without giving himself time to think, Paul scrambled down the rocks towards the edge of the breaking sea. Almost within reach now. Her arm swung, and the line slithered into the water well short of where he stood. He began to go forward, saw the breaking sea at the last moment and scuttled back while the water surged round his knees and almost to his waist. Hand over hand she pulled the line in and then, as the boat came abreast of him, threw it again.

This time it pitched almost over his shoulder. He ran it round him under his armpits, threw a pair of half-hitches round the standing end, gulped a mouthful of air and plunged face down into the retreating sea. For a moment or two he struck out desperately and then found himself sliding down into a gulf of water. Down and down he went and then felt, as he had felt before, the enormous thrust of the water under him as the sea lifted him bodily on its crest to throw him backwards on to the rocks. For a moment he hung on the crest and heard himself scream uselessly in the grip of the sea. Then, with a jerk that nearly kicked the breath out of him, the line took the strain and held him. At first physical pain overcame his fear as the line tightened ferociously round his chest and the sea pulled at his trailing body. Then the wave went from under him. The line slackened momentarily, and as he struck out wildly towards the boat he heard behind him the roar of the bursting sea.

He was all right now. He knew what he must do now. Comfort rose in him again and he began to think more clearly. Steadily the distance closed, as the line drew him and he put out what was left of his strength. The white topsides of the boat were suddenly above him. He grabbed once and missed, and then at a second try got first one hand and then the other over the gunwale and clung.

Susan made the line fast and came to him. She put her hands under his arms and the two of them struggled as the boat lurched through the sea. Cardew said, 'You take her for a moment, Sue. I'll get him in. Keep her head to the sea. That's all. If you don't we'll all be in the drink together. Keep her going steady and for Christ's sake don't let her turn across the sea.'

Susan nodded and went to him. 'Ready?' he said. She nodded again and took the wheel.

Cardew ran forward. 'Now,' he said. He heaved with surprising strength and Paul gripped and pulled. For a moment his weight hung over the gunwale of the heeling boat and then he pitched head first inboard. Cardew left him where he lay and ran back to the wheel.

'Good girl,' he said. 'I've got her.'

The engine picked up and the buff white bows bit strongly into the crests of the advancing seas. Susan wrestled with the sodden knot and suddenly the constriction round his chest eased. Paul crawled into the bows and sat on the floor boards, his head between his knees. Then he looked up.

'You're quite a sailor, Sue,' he said.

CHAPTER TWENTY

'Whichever way you look at it,' said the sergeant, 'what our sportsman wanted was to stop you getting down to the bottom. And Mrs Trent, too, by the looks of it, if it was her shoe you saw. Whether he'd have put a bullet through you rather than let you get down we can't say. Of course, if he could drown you without drilling a hole in you, so much the better for him. That's what he meant to do, I'd say – knock you off the rock into the sea, as he did Mrs Trent, in the hope that you wouldn't get out alive any more than she did. Of course, he'd reckon on your being a much stronger swimmer, but the conditions was much worse. I'd say it was the wind saved you, sir, even if it did come near drowning you to make up. If conditions had been calm, he wouldn't have risked letting you go. He'd have put a bullet in you at once, and perhaps hoped to get hold of the body before it was washed up somewhere. What we don't know is whether he knows you got out alive. It wouldn't have been easy for him, even if he stayed watching, to keep track of you in that sea, not from the top of the cliff. Anyway, as I see it, the first thing we've got to do is find out what's at the bottom of that path. If we know what there is to hide, we shouldn't be in much doubt who's trying to hide it.'

'There's another point,' said Paul. 'How did he know I was there at all? Or Mrs Trent, for that matter. There won't be many people find that path. Whoever it is interested in it, he can't keep a permanent watch on it. Unless his interest is only occasional. Mrs Trent and I may have had the bad luck to go down in the close season.'

' 'Tis possible. Where was the tide when you went in, now?'

'Near half-ebb,' said Paul.

'So it would be. 'Tis different now – an hour past low water, and starting to make fast. But whatever there is to see, we should still be able to see it, if we don't waste time.'

He pulled the black car off the road and got out. The second car pulled in behind and Paul saw that one of the constables carried ropes. When they came to the stile, Paul said, 'Who put that notice up? Mr Bannerman, I imagine?'

'Mr Bannerman it would be, yes, sir. Very particular about his property, as you'll have seen.'

'He seems to be wrong on one point, anyhow. It seems that there is a way down to the sea. But I wouldn't deny that the cliffs are dangerous.'

'It would seem he didn't know the path down was there. You say it isn't easy to see, and I certainly never knew there was one.'

'Yes. I shouldn't have seen it if – if I hadn't been looking for it. I knew,' he went on quickly, 'that Mrs Trent couldn't have fallen from the top, or she'd have been much more smashed up. And as everybody seemed to agree that

184

she must have gone in somewhere on Bartenny, I reckoned she must have got at least part of the way down before she went in. There had to be a path of some sort. All this bit is sheer drop. It's only out at the end of the head that the cliffs do slope out a bit, and as you'll see, it's there in fact the way down is. But so far as Mr Bannerman's concerned, he told me himself there wasn't one.'

'Yes. Well, that's his notice and that's what it says. Now, sir. What I have in mind is this. You say there's only one place on the coastguard path where you can see the path down at the particular place where you were shot at. Therefore you say the shots must have been fired from there. Now I reckon we'd better first check that – go right round the path and make sure there's no other place he could have fired from. Then if we're satisfied on that, we'll leave a couple of men at that point, and you and me'll go down where you went yesterday. That's if you won't mind, sir. I've brought ropes, as you see, in case they're needed. Apart from anything else, from what you say we may need them if we're going to get hold of that shoe.'

'I'm willing,' said Paul. 'I can be as brave as the next man with the police keeping me company.'

'Good. Let's get on then, sir.'

They climbed the stile and set out along the path. The wind had blown itself out, and there was no more than a mild breeze. Such as it was, it still blew from the west, driving the long swell the wind had left. Sky and sea were a uniform grey, and Paul was conscious of a chill in the air that felt like the first breath of autumn.

They came to the end of the wire fence, Paul and the sergeant in the lead, with two constables behind them and the third, carrying the ropes, bringing up the rear. Clothed with bracken and gorse and topped by its coronet of splintered rock, Bartenny Head stood up ahead of them.

Paul did not see the flash, but it was from up among the rocks, he thought, that the first shot came. The bullet sang viciously off a rock on their left and whined away out over the sea.

Everybody stopped dead. There was a second shot, and the constable at the rear said 'Cor' and dropped, white-faced, to his knees. They threw themselves into the cover of gorse and rock. 'Edwards!' said the sergeant. 'Are you all right, man?'

From behind his rock they heard the constable swallow twice. 'I'm all right,' he said. 'It's me helmet. Shot clean through at the top.'

The sergeant whistled softly. 'So long as it's not your head,' he said. 'Anyone see where he's shooting from?'

'Not for certain. Up in the rocks, I'd reckon.'

The other constable agreed. 'He's up there somewhere all right.' Constable Edwards offered no opinion.

'Right,' said the sergeant. 'Ferrar, you were in the army, weren't you?'

'No, sergeant. Air Force.'

'Well there. Sorry we left our aeroplanes. But it's the same principle. You make your way along to the right. Crawl, do you see? Doesn't matter how long it takes you, but don't stick your head up. Or anything else for that matter. But go on until you get to the path on the other side. Stay there, under cover, mind, but watch that path. If you see anyone coming along it from the head, yell blue murder. Or don't yell, blow your whistle. Sounds better. If you can't help yourself, stop whoever it is, but try not to get killed doing it. We'll all be on the way the moment you start blowing.'

Constable Ferrar started on his journey.

'There's one thing,' said Paul, 'we know the answer to one of our questions. He knows I got out of the sea alive,

Nothing else would explain this sort of reception, surely.'

'It could be. But he may always have been keeping watch, like, from the top there. And seeing our party, he'd know he couldn't do what he's done before, so he opens up at long range, like. But I can't see what he's at, all the same. He can't hold out there indefinitely. We can bring up the military if we have to. Then what's he gaining, do you reckon, holding us up like this?'

'Time, one would think,' said Paul. 'But time for what I don't know.'

'No more do I. What could he be waiting for, now?'

'Rescue, possibly. But it would have to be by sea, unless we're going to be attacked in the rear by superior forces, which I can't really think likely. That's ruling out anything exotic, like helicopters. But I suppose it's just possible someone might pick him up in a boat, if he could get down to the water. He's only got to get as far as I did yesterday and then jump or dive for it. In these conditions there'd be no trouble about picking him up if the boat was standing by. He may be just holding us up till it comes. For that matter, it could be already under the head. We couldn't see it from here. And we couldn't see him going down to it. Assuming he's up on top of the head, he could slip down the far side and down the path at any time without our knowing, while he's got our heads down here. The only way we can be certain he's still there is if he fires.'

'That's so,' said the sergeant. He stood up. A bullet within a foot on each side of him brought him down with a thud breathing heavily through his nose. 'It would seem he's still there,' he said.

'That's automatic fire,' said Paul. 'It's also, I suspect, very careful and accurate shooting. It's what he did to me yesterday. I don't think he wants to kill anybody if he can help it. But I shouldn't like to push him too far, I don't think. It still looks like playing for time, though.'

'I've been thinking,' said the sergeant. 'Apart from the possibility of rescue, there's two things happening. The daylight's running out, but so slowly he can hardly hope to hold out till dark. And the tide's making. That's much quicker. Supposing there's something down there the tide will cover when it gets high enough. He's got a real chance of holding us up till then. The tide was falling when you went down, wasn't it, now? And if you remember, it would have been the same when Mrs Trent went down – that's if she went down. Supposing this joker won't have anyone go down the path without there's enough tide to suit his purposes, whatever they are?'

A fusillade apparently aimed at the eastern leg of the path showed that Constable Ferrar's movements had not gone unobserved. The sergeant swore under his breath. 'I hope that boy's all right,' he said. 'Jackson, move over under cover to a point about half-way between Ferrar and me, so's you'll be within earshot of both of us. Find out where he is and if he's all right, and pass word back to me, will you? Edwards, you all right?'

'I'm all right, sergeant.'

'Good. You move over about half-way between Jackson and me. I want to get us spread right out across the head, see? He can't shoot at five of us simultaneous. Keep your ropes on you. We may need them yet.'

Edwards, led by his pierced helmet and followed by coils of rope, went painfully after Jackson. Presently Jackson's voice came across the gorse bushes. 'Sergeant!' he yelled.

'Hullo?'

'Ferrar's on the path and he's all right. He says the shooting is from between the two big rocks at the top.'

'Right. Now, sir.' He turned to Paul, who shared his

gorse bush. 'We've got to move in on this joker. I agree with you, he probably won't hurt anyone if he can help it, but if he finds he's getting pressed, he may not be so careful. I don't think I'd trust him too far, either. He may not have shot you yesterday, but he didn't exactly hurry to pull you out of the sea, did he? All right. Now so far as we're concerned, it's our job and we take the risk as part of it. But that doesn't apply to you. You've had one nasty passage, and I'd as lief you didn't run any further risk. If you come on with us now, you'll do it on your own responsibility. I don't mind saying we can do with an extra man, because the more we are, the safer we are. But it's entirely up to you. I'm not calling on you officially to assist the police in an affair like this.'

'I'm coming,' said Paul. 'I understand the position, of course.'

'Right, sir.' He raised his voice. 'Jackson. Edwards.' Two gorse bushes about twenty yards apart acknowledged the signal. 'We're all going forward together when I give three short blasts. Keep under cover as much as possible and take it slow and careful. 'Tisn't like a cavalry charge. But keep moving up. If I give one long blast, stay where you are and await orders. And keep your eyes skinned. Our man may try to break out any time. Pass that on to Ferrar, will you, Jackson?'

They heard Jackson's voice passing the order of battle out to the right flank. Then he called, 'Sergeant? Ferrar's O.K.'

'Right,' said the sergeant. He put his whistle to his lips and blew three short blasts. The sound drifted away eastwards on the breeze, and the advance began. Strung out across the rough slope, creeping and dodging, swearing and panting, the party moved in on Bartenny Head. It was slow work. Any visible movement was fired on, but not

189

even an automatic rifle can cover five separate lines of advance.

The ground became steeper and, what was worse, clearer. It was getting more difficult to move under cover, and Paul became aware of a new malice in the shooting. Once as he lay flat a bullet tore through the gorse bush inches above his head, and he found himself shamefacedly reluctant to make a fresh move. In fact his next move went unmolested, but there was a simultaneous burst of firing against the far end of the line. Almost at once he heard Constable Jackson shouting from the middle station.

'Sergeant,' he called, 'Ferrar's been hit.'

A long blast halted the advance. 'Go over to him and report back,' the sergeant shouted.

Paul looked at his watch and saw with surprise how long the advance had taken. The tide would be near the half-flood now, he thought; and suddenly knew what the battle was about.

Constable Jackson's voice said, 'He's hit in the shoulder, sergeant. High up. It's bleeding, of course, but he'll be all right.'

'Tell him to stay where he is,' the sergeant said, but Paul was on his feet shouting. 'There he goes,' he said.

A figure, dun-coloured and featureless, ran crouching among the rocks ahead and his pursuers were up and after him. Paul, on the westward leg of the path, found himself in a clear lead, but could hear the sergeant pounding along not far behind. For several seconds their quarry vanished and then, as he came round a bend, Paul saw him again. He was poised on the brink of the cliff and as Paul watched he swung and threw something that fell in a long glittering curve towards the sea. Then he was off again, heading east.

Paul wondered whether Jackson had had the sense to

take the eastern path in place of the injured Ferrar. He looked to his right, but the high ground of the head towered over him, and neither Jackson nor Edwards could be seen. He came to the green slope above the gorse bushes, but wherever his man had gone, he could not have gone down the path to the Glyn. He ran on and as he ran heard shouting ahead. The hunt was closing in. The eastern path was blocked, and the constables there had seen their man.

Paul rounded a bend and saw Jackson, still at some distance, running up the path to meet him. For a moment blank incredulity engulfed him. Then the constable shouted, pointing down the slope, and Paul saw what had happened. Their quarry had left the coastguard path and turned back along the edge of the cliff. He was already below Paul and not twenty yards from the top of the Glyn path.

Paul stopped and turned in his tracks. The sergeant came round the bend, saw Paul's pointing hand and stopped too. Below them the grey figure, still muffled, leapt suddenly and breath-takingly from one rock to another, scrambled across a shelving slope of thin turf, missed its footing and started, inexorably and horribly, to roll. It scrabbled for a moment with bare hands at the lip of the rock, jerked backwards and was gone. Paul sat down suddenly on the path and put his head between his knees. He struggled to keep hold of his senses as the police closed round him shouting.

They made fast their ropes and swung them out over the edge of the cliff, but Paul knew what he must do. He went back along the path, down the green slope and through the over-growing gorse-bushes. For the second time he started down the path to the Glyn, but did not expect, even this time, to complete the journey. Bannerman lay perfectly still on the path. His mask was off and he was smiling as Paul came down to him. He answered Paul's questions with a sort of humorous detachment and died, still smiling, as the sergeant came down the cliff on his rope.

'Sergeant,' said Paul.

'Sir?'

'I need your help urgently.' He produced a document from an inner pocket and offered it for the sergeant's inspection.

'Ah,' he said. 'So that's it. What do you want done, then, sir?'

'I want you to get me to a telephone as quick as you can manage it.'

It was almost dark when the *Autolycus* crept on to her moorings on the last of the flood and sat there heavily. She was well down in the water, Mr Menloe noticed. He watched Mr Gerard batten down and lock up with his usual care and come ashore in his dinghy with a breathtaking silver-gilt woman, who was silent and quite white, as if the remnants of the swell had not agreed with her. Mr Menloe approved. He liked a bit of vicarious immorality in cabin-cruisers, and Mr Gerard certainly knew what he was about with this one. He heard faintly, but did not see, the police cars that, at the top of the cliff, drew themselves up so as to block the only road out of Cainport.

CHAPTER TWENTY-ONE

'I owe you an apology,' said Paul. 'But you know, I really did come down here on holiday, and I had no idea things would turn out as they have. I assumed, as we all did, that Mrs Trent's death was an accident. And even if it wasn't, it didn't seem any concern of mine. There was this business which, as we now know, Bannerman was involved in – I'll talk about that in a minute. But there was nothing, at first anyhow, to connect Mrs Trent with that, and I'm afraid my one idea was to keep out. It was only later that some sort of connection seemed probable. If I'd thought things would go as they have, I'd have declared my interest much sooner.'

'That's all right, sir. I understand that, and I can't say I blame you.' The sergeant paused. 'You never got down to the cave, sir, did you?'

'Ah – you found the cave, did you?'

'That's right, sir. As soon as we'd settled the other business, we went down the path as we'd meant to do when we first got there. We found the shoe all right. It hasn't been formally identified yet, but I'd say there was no doubt it was Mrs Trent's. Then at the bottom of the path there's a biggish cave that none of us knew was there, nor anyone else we've asked so far. The sea was well into it when we got down, but it must empty pretty well at low water. Whether you could get a boat in we don't yet know. It don't look as if it was possible, but we'll have to go into that. There wasn't nothing of significance anywhere. But the cave had been used all right. There was an upper part, well above the high-water mark, that didn't hardly show at all. We only found it because we had lights and were looking for something of the sort. It's been levelled off into a sort of platform, with a bit of concrete work here and there, and by the look of it has been used for storage of some kind. All we found was tarpaulins and some ropes and an empty packing case. But it would hold a fair amount of stuff.'

'It had held stuff,' said Paul. 'And I think you'll find you can get a boat in. They were loading it, of course, while Bannerman was fighting his rearguard action. But I'd better begin at the beginning. Bannerman – that wasn't his real name, by the way – was a member of a pretty high-powered organisation that specialised in the disposal of stuff the ordinary men couldn't handle – looted works of art, special jewellery and that sort of thing – stuff that was known and had a history. There was a lot lost in the war, you know, all over the Continent, that's never been found and that couldn't be sold in the ordinary way – or broken up without destroying its value. Buyers can be found for that sort of stuff, but you need a very big organisation and you've got to have time. The organisations were there after the war, but they gradually got rounded up or went out of business. There was only one that just dropped out of sight, and among its known members was our friend Bannerman.'

'Ah.' The sergeant smiled ruefully. 'You as good as told me he wasn't what he seemed to be, and I was for defending him. But you've got to see the thing from our point of view, sir. We're not secret police or security forces. So long as a man is respectable and pays his rates and taxes and doesn't make trouble with his neighbours, we can't go looking for explanations if he chooses to do things his own way, nor we can't go asking where he gets his money from. Bannerman – let's call him that, anyway – bought the place after the war and started in farming. He didn't pretend he wasn't new to it, but there was many in the same position then. And there's no question he worked at it and in the end he made it pay. He was a good farmer and a good employer. Of course, you could see he had money behind him, but as I say, that's no crime, and it wasn't for us to ask where it come from.'

'My dear chap, I know that. My position was quite different. It's not my department, but it seems they'd known for some time that there was a way out of the country for stuff of this class – and of course, there's fresh stuff coming on the market all the time, pictures especially, as you know – and they'd lately begun to suspect that the key point might be down in these parts. I was told this when they knew I was coming down here. Obviously I had no official charge in the matter, but they mentioned it in case anything caught my eye. And of course Bannerman caught my eye. He walked right into it. He didn't know who I was, naturally. I still think he was an extraordinary chap. I think he saw, when it was too late, that I was taking the wrong sort of interest in him. But you see, the key to the whole thing was a cast-iron safe-deposit of some sort, and Bannerman was at pains to show me there wasn't one. I stumbled by pure chance on the Cainport connection. But the cave was the vital thing – and it was Mrs Trent, as you might say, who led me there. Or put me on the road, anyhow. Bannerman saw to it that I never got there, but only at the cost of blowing the whole thing sky high.'

'What was he then, originally, sir?'

Paul smiled. 'His father was a Jewish tailor in Stepney. The name was Levi.'

'Levi,' said the sergeant. 'You wouldn't hardly credit it, would you? And he'd have been on the Bench and a member of the Joint Standing Committee in no time.'

Paul nodded. 'And a very useful member, too. It makes you think, doesn't it? All he wanted to give him value, real value, was a proper income. And just because his source of income was technically inadmissible, the whole man's wasted. And I bet you he appreciated the stuff he was handling far more than most of the legal owners.'

Bannerman, thought Paul, Bannerman with his tall distinction and his clipped officer's speech. Bannerman with his perfect clothes and his beautiful house. Bannerman with his exquisite food and wine and his silver-gilt nymphs. Even Bannerman with his Jersey calves and his devoted Labradors. Bannerman who loved it all so genuinely, but couldn't help, once in a while, having somebody see how perfect it all was and how much he loved it. He sighed, and found the sergeant looking at him curiously.

'It's no good,' he said, 'I liked him, you know. I could almost wish he'd got away with it.'

The sergeant offered no comment. Instead he said, 'Where did he learn to shoot like that, I wonder?'

'Ah, that would have been in the Army. He was a specialist at one time – weapons training and so on. He did very well for himself in the war, but I fancy didn't see much fighting. He was in Europe at the end and must have got mixed up in the business then. There was all sorts going on, as you know. Then he got himself out of the Army, changed his name and before many years were out had more than one police force interested in him. But as I say, no one ever caught up with him or any of his lot, except some of the small men.'

The sergeant nodded. 'And then he comes down here, as we know, after the war. Somebody must have known about the cave, I suppose, and bought the place on purpose. And here he's been ever since, and I suppose playing his part in the business all the time and getting paid off accordingly.'

'And doing what he'd always wanted to do. Leading the good life according to his lights. And not a bad one according to anyone's. It's no good, sergeant. I wish he'd got away with it.'

'I don't know about the good life, sir. That's for you to judge. He killed Mrs Trent. He came near killing you.

He put a bullet in young Ferrar. How would you reckon that up?'

'We trespassed on his preserves. And – yes, of course I admit the ruthlessness. He'd have done anything to keep things as they were.'

The sergeant continued to look at him with a mild and speculative eye. He said, 'You was lucky to have young Cardew come round in his boat that day, wasn't you, sir? Not many boats out that day, I reckon.'

'I was lucky all right. But it wasn't all that of a sea, you know, for a boat of that sort. And Cardew knows the waters round here better than most, I gather.'

'That's so,' said the sergeant. 'If his dad taught him all he knew, he knows this bit of coast better than anyone, I reckon.' He paused. 'Still,' he went on, 'I suppose you had had your bit of bad luck, in a manner of speaking, finding the path down like you did. And Mrs Trent the same.' He paused again. 'You know Cardew was out Bartenny way the day she went in? Only he never saw her, poor lady. Of course, she wasn't any swimmer by all accounts.'

There was a moment's silence. Then Paul said, 'Oh, I know one thing I wanted to ask you. How did Bannerman – I won't call him anything else – how did Bannerman know I was going down the path – or Mrs Trent either, for that matter? He can't have kept a permanent watch. You can't see the top of the path from the house anyway. Or had he got a look-out posted?'

'No, sir. There's an alarm bell in the house that rings if anyone goes down the path.'

'But how—? Not one of those ray things that open doors before you come to them?'

'No, sir, no. Nothing fancy like that. Just a contact wire, like they have at garages. You know – rings a bell inside when your car goes over it and the chap stops doing his pools and comes out and serves you, that's if you're lucky. We found the bell ringing, as a matter of fact, after we'd come up the path and couldn't see what else it was for. So we traced the connection clear of the buildings on a line towards the head. Then we stopped the bell with the cut-out switch and I sent one of my chaps down the path again, and sure enough the bell started up. After that it wasn't hard to find. There's flat stone right across the path at the top, half under the gorse. You can't help but tread on it, and that rings the bell in the house. And that gave anybody time to get along to the top of the path before whoever it was was well down it. Of course, Bannerman can't always have been there, though he wasn't away much, but I suppose they had something worked out. He can't have been quite single-handed. There was a woman working for him we haven't found. She may have been one of them. But after all, this wasn't more than an emergency arrangement. I wouldn't be surprised if Mrs Trent wasn't the first to set it off.'

'I wonder if Ah – if his assistant was as handy with a gun as he was? On the whole I'm glad he was at home when I went down. He missed me very accurately. Well, you had some of his shooting later.'

'Yes, sir.' He paused and eyed Paul again. 'To go back to what we were saying, sir, if you'll excuse me. About young Cardew.' He shifted the papers in front of him and seemed to be searching among them for the words he wanted. Without moving his head he flicked his eyes up suddenly to Paul's face and for a moment the two men looked at each other. He said, 'I don't question your position, sir. I know Cardew's honest. Mrs Trent I never knew, poor lady, but whatever her faults may have been, she didn't have anything to do with Bannerman. Now, sir. I don't want to make unnecessary trouble anywhere, particularly now, so far as young Cardew's concerned. It don't matter, in fact, what took Mrs Trent down the path, or who she was going to meet, if there was anybody. All that matters is that she went down the path and so – what was your expression, now? – trespassed on Bannerman's preserves. The results we know. But she did it unconscious, and so far as Bannerman's case is concerned, it doesn't matter that I can see what she did have in mind. In your case you were, so to say, following Mrs Trent's movements to see if you could find out what happened to her. And you found out, pretty sharp. So I don't see it matters, even if I do get the feeling that there's a thing or two still not fully explained. But I think the better you and I understand one another, the better it is all round. There won't be any court case come of Mrs Trent's death, after all. Bannerman's dead, and Mrs Trent's dead and you're luckily none the worse. So far as that's concerned, the case is closed pretty well. Only, as I said, I didn't want to feel we didn't understand one another.'

Paul said, 'Thank you, sergeant. You take a considerable weight off my mind. And yes, I think we understand each other very well. Like you, I'm rather anxious not to make trouble for Cardew just now. You see that, don't you?'

'That's right, sir. I know. Only, as I say, so long as you and I understand one another.' He got up. 'You're off tomorrow, I take it?'

'We are, yes. With rather mixed feelings all round.'

'Ah, I can understand that. Most of the Carrack's visitors going this week-end, too, I'm told?'

'I expect so. I know Colonel Frayne and his family are.'

'Yes, sir, so I believe.'

'Do you know Charles, in the Carrack's front bar?'

199

'I know of him, sir, of course. I can't say I've spoken to him.'

'You should,' said Paul. 'You'd find it interesting. He must know almost as much about what's going on as you do.'

'Is that so, sir? I'll remember that next time we have any trouble. That's if we do. Good-bye, sir. I hope we see you here next year, despite everything.'

They shook hands. 'You may yet,' said Paul.

'Next year?' said Charles. 'I well might. It will be my last long vac. before finals.'

'It will be your last chance to get that book written.'

Charles smiled. 'I can't write it if the facts keep going wrong.'

'You think they have?'

'Apparently. Grossly wrong. For Mrs Trent to have been killed at a distance, casually, by a man who never knew her doesn't make sense. It doesn't fit any possible picture of her. It would have been all right if it had happened to you. I mean artistically right. I'm glad it didn't, of course. But with Mrs Trent it's nonsense.'

'Me not being potentially a tragic figure?'

'Good God, no. You don't want to be, do you? You're the audience. You're detached. You're immune from the forces that drive the characters. You're all right provided the theatre doesn't catch fire and you don't get run over on the way home.'

'It doesn't sound very heroic.'

'Who wants heroism?' said Charles.

Paul said, 'Is Mr Dawson about, do you know?'

'Dawson? He's gone – they went this morning. They had one last monumental row. I don't know what started it. Then he did some pretty steady farewell drinking in here last night, and this morning they took themselves off to the connubial home. It hardly bears thinking about, does it? But of course, he'll be happier back at the office. They oughtn't really to go on holiday at all.'

'It's the sailing,' said Paul. 'At least she lets him do that – in suitable company.'

'She did until the Mrs Trent business. I wonder whether she will in future? It's his last source of happiness, you see. She's bound to find it a temptation.'

Paul thought. 'Is there an address?' he said.

Charles looked at him curiously. 'All the addresses are in the book,' he said.

'So they are. Well there. Till next year, perhaps, Charles.'

'Perhaps.' He smiled radiantly, but they did not shake hands.

CHAPTER TWENTY-TWO

The wind howled dismally and flung a handful of rain against the hotel window. Charles's bar had reverted to what the management called a Residents' Lounge. There were heavy curtains and a coal fire. Paul sat back in his chair and watched the flames.

The door opened quietly and Major Trent came in. For a moment Paul hardly recognised him. He wore a dark suit and had taken off a lot of weight. He moved more easily. But it was in the face that the difference lay. It had lost its rigidity and the eyes no longer stared. He smiled, and there was no mistaking the gaiety. He said, 'Hullo, Mycroft,' and sat in one of the other two chairs.

Paul said, 'I'm glad you could come.'

'Glad, are you? Well – your letter gave me no alter-

201

native. But I come with a very open mind.'

'So do I. Dawson's coming. Did you know?'

He nodded. 'They told me. I thought we had an inquest at the time.'

Paul remembered the granite hall and the stifled sunlight. 'It's not an inquest,' he said. 'So far as I'm concerned it's more an exorcism. I found I couldn't leave things as they were. Between us, I mean. Only between us.'

'And Dawson, presumably?'

'And Dawson, yes.'

Major Trent said, 'I've ordered a bottle of whisky and a syphon. Is that in order? You're in the chair.'

Paul nodded, and a man came in with a tray. Major Trent poured out two stiff ones. 'We'll leave half the bottle for Dawson,' he said. 'That should put us on an even footing.' He waved his glass. 'Happy days,' he said. He said it perfectly seriously.

Paul said, 'My letter must have reached you. Are you still at Tonbridge? Or is it the west coast of Scotland?'

'I said the west coast, did I? No, as a matter of fact it's Ireland, but the principle's the same.' He drank again. 'I'm sorry about Bannerman,' he said.

'So am I,' said Paul.

'Are you?' He laughed. 'That's nice of you, considering.'

'He couldn't help himself,' said Paul. 'He had the right instincts.'

'I've got his dogs.'

'You've – what?'

'I've got his dogs. No one else wanted them, and I owed Bannerman a good turn. They missed him at first, of course, but they're settling down. They're nice beasts, and it's a good place for them.'

'Well I'm damned.' Paul drank and found a ridiculous difficulty in swallowing.

Major Trent said, 'I wonder how Dawson's managing it?'

'To get here? Some sort of a business trip, I imagine. Only I don't know what his business is.'

'Insurance. Might just do. I hope your wife isn't worried.'

'A bit doubtful, but open to persuasion.'

The wind howled outside the shut windows, and they refilled their glasses and drank again. The door opened, and Dawson stood in the doorway, looking from one to the other.

Major Trent said, 'Come on, Dawson. You're two rounds behind. Unless you already have the advantage of us.'

Dawson shut the door behind him, but still stood there. He had lost his tan, but his office suit improved him. His face was drawn and wary. He said, 'What the hell are you doing here, Trent?'

Major Trent shrugged. 'Ask Mycroft,' he said. 'He's master of ceremonies. He says it's an exorcism. You can make what you like of that.'

Dawson sat down rather heavily in the third chair. He clearly had the advantage of them. It looked a considerable advantage. Paul remembered very vividly their conversation in the small room next door, but it seemed a very long time ago.

Dawson said, 'Well, what's all this about?'

Paul said, 'Have a drink first, if Trent doesn't mind.' Dawson poured himself a thick one almost without taking his eyes off Paul's face. They all drank, but this time no one said anything.

Paul said, 'Mrs Trent went into the sea off the end of Bartenny. We must assume Bannerman shot at her, as he later shot at me.'

Major Trent said, 'What was she doing out there? Or rather, who was she meeting? Not Bannerman, presumably?'

'That's not known. But no, almost certainly not Bannerman. That wouldn't fit.'

Major Trent said, 'Well?'

'It was fine weather, and warm. There was an almost flat sea. There was the tide-run, of course, that would have taken her straight down towards the river mouth.'

Major Trent said, 'She could hardly swim at all, you know. And the sea frightened her. She wouldn't have stayed afloat long.'

'She'd have stayed afloat indefinitely,' said Paul. 'She had a life-jacket on.'

'What makes you think that?'

'I know, as it happens.'

'How do you know?'

'Bannerman told me.'

'Ah. Bannerman told you, did he? Why and when?'

'Because I asked him. Just before he died.'

Major Trent nodded. He drank and refilled his glass.

Dawson sat slumped in his chair looking from one to the other. Suddenly he sat up. 'Of course she had,' he said. His voice was hoarse but perfectly clear. 'I saw her.'

Paul said, 'I thought you must have.'

Major Trent said, 'Well – I'm – damned. Poor old Jolly Jack,' and Dawson turned on him with a snarl.

'What the hell do you mean by that?' he said.

Major Trent shrugged. 'My sympathy is perfectly genuine,' he said.

Dawson slumped back in his chair, and for a minute no one spoke. Then he said, 'I was out there, single-handed.' His voice was barely audible. He roused himself, but did not look at either of them. 'I was reaching against the ebb.

The breeze was northerly, what there was of it. I was sailing across Lanting, but my time was running out. I had – I had told Agnes when I should be back, and she was going to meet me and help me get the boat in. I thought I heard someone call. It was to leeward, between me and the land. It was – she was masked by the mainsail, of course. I looked under the boom, as one does, and I saw her. She was some way off, but it was her all right. She was floating face up, not swimming, but floating with her head quite high out of the water. There was no sea to speak of, only the tide-run. I only got a glimpse of her, but I could see the jacket. She couldn't have known I'd seen her. I put the helm down and turned into the wind.'

He stopped suddenly and seemed to notice the glass in his hand. He tilted his head back and poured the neat spirit straight down. He did not appear to swallow at all. He sat up and spoke quite loud and distinctly. He said, 'Then I went about and sailed back across the river mouth. It was still masked by the sail, of course.'

No one said anything. The gusts still howled against the windows, but the rain seemed to have stopped. Major Trent reached out very deliberately and poured himself another tot. He offered the bottle to Paul, but he shook his head.

Paul said, 'She should have got ashore all right.'

'Good God,' said Dawson, 'of course she should have. There was nothing to stop her. I came in when – when I had said I would and we got the boat in and I came back here. I heard – I forget, I think someone said she was missing, but I kept on expecting her to turn up.' His voice wobbled and for a horrifying moment Paul thought he was going to cry. Instead he swallowed hard and sat staring at the fire. He said, 'You may think—' but Paul cut him short.

205

'No,' he said. 'What we think isn't in question. It's only the facts I wanted. I had to know. I'm sorry to have to dig it up.'

Major Trent said, 'Don't worry. Dawson's not done himself any harm by telling us.' He spoke lightly but perfectly kindly.

'You don't know what the hell you're talking about,' said Dawson. He swivelled in his chair and said to Paul, 'I thought at first she must have drowned in spite of it. She could, I suppose, if she fainted and then turned over on her face. Then when I heard she hadn't a jacket on when you found her, I wondered if I could have been mistaken. But I knew I couldn't have. Anyway, don't you see, she'd never have got where I saw her without one, not alive. Trent knows that. No, she – she must have got it off her somehow. I don't know.'

Paul looked at Major Trent. Major Trent looked at Dawson. Then he turned to Paul and shrugged. 'You know,' he said, 'don't you? She had it on, all right. I took it off.'

Dawson did not move anything but his eyes. They turned and fixed Major Trent with a curious blind stare. He said almost under his breath, 'You – what?'

'I took it off. I was out single-handed that evening, too, you know. I saw you go about, but I never thought, even afterwards, that you could have seen her. I assumed no one had. Well, naturally, or I probably shouldn't have done what I did. She didn't call out to me. I came on her, not far out off Lanting. She was floating, as you said, but she was barely conscious. I imagine it was exhaustion and shock generally. She wasn't – she hadn't got her face in the water at all. I remember noticing that her hair was wet, but her make-up was in good order. Her eyes were shut, but she was breathing all right. There was no one anywhere near. I leant out and grabbed her. The boat came up into the wind. She opened her eyes but didn't seem to take much in. I unlaced her jacket. I couldn't have got it over her head and arms, not without upsetting the boat. Just when I'd got it undone she opened her eyes very wide and we looked at each other. She knew it was me. She didn't say anything. I rolled her over and pulled the jacket off her. Then I just let her go. She slid back into the water and a moment later went under quite quietly. I doubt if she knew much about it. I was well up-river before I realised I had still got her jacket in the boat. There was nothing I could do then but take it back with me. I got rid of it, of course, but' – he smiled at Paul – 'not quite soon enough.'

He turned to Dawson. 'So you've nothing to worry about, Dawson. So far as you were concerned, she'd have been all right. Only I drowned her. Well, she was my wife, you know. Or don't you? No, on consideration, of course you don't. I expect you thought you knew her. So did a lot of other people, but they weren't married to her either.' He turned to Paul. 'I wish I could give you a proper picture of Millie,' he said, 'but I won't try, I don't think.'

He got up. 'Well,' he said, 'is the exorcism complete?'

Dawson said, 'But what are we going to do?'

'Do?' said Major Trent. 'Nothing, obviously. There's nothing to be done. Millie would have been alive if someone hadn't sent her out to Bartenny, or if Bannerman hadn't shot her into the sea, or if you hadn't left her in it, or if I hadn't taken her jacket off. But she's dead, Dawson, and there's nothing can be done. And none of this will go any further. Mycroft won't talk and I certainly won't. And I don't think you will. And there's no evidence in any case. All right, Mycroft?' Paul nodded. 'Right. Then I'll be off. I don't think I'll stay the night.' He smiled suddenly.

'They've given me No. 23. Not very imaginative.'

He nodded to Paul and went out. Dawson did not move. Paul walked out of the hotel and across to the sea-wall. The wind had blown the sky clear of cloud and there was a young moon going down across a flooded river. He leant on his elbows and said, 'Millie, Millie, Millie, Millie' to the water under the wall. Millie and the men around her. Four men at the end. The younger man she loved, and the older man who loved her, and the man who didn't know her at all, and the man who knew her too well. It was like fortunes by cards. One at your head, one at your feet, one at your right hand, one at your left. The man who didn't know her shot her off her rock into the sea. The man she loved looked for her and could not find her. The man who loved her found her and let her go. So the man who knew her found her. And he took and drowned her like a kitten.

He shivered violently and realised, even through the whisky, that it was bitterly cold after the warmth of Charles's bar. He turned and went back into the hotel.

〉〉〉 If you've enjoyed this book and would like to discover more great vintage crime and thriller titles, as well as the most exciting crime and thriller authors writing today, visit: 〉〉〉

The Murder Room
Where Criminal Minds Meet

themurderroom.com